Time is
running out...

For Ash—
welcome to the family!—Jack Heath

Scholastic Australia
An imprint of Scholastic Australia Pty Limited
PO Box 579 Gosford NSW 2250
ABN 11 000 614 577
www.scholastic.com.au

Part of the Scholastic Group
Sydney • Auckland • New York • Toronto • London • Mexico City
New Delhi • Hong Kong • Buenos Aires • Puerto Rico

Published by Scholastic Australia in 2019.

A catalogue record for this book is available from the National Library of Australia

ISBN: 978-1-74299-343-0

Typeset in Versailles LT.

Printed in China by Hang Tai Printing Company Limited.

This product is made of material from well-managed FSC®-certified forests, recycled material, and other controlled sources.

10 9 8 7 6 5 4 3 2 1 26 27 28 29 30 / 2

LIARS

ARMAGEDDON

JACK HEATH

A Scholastic Australia Book

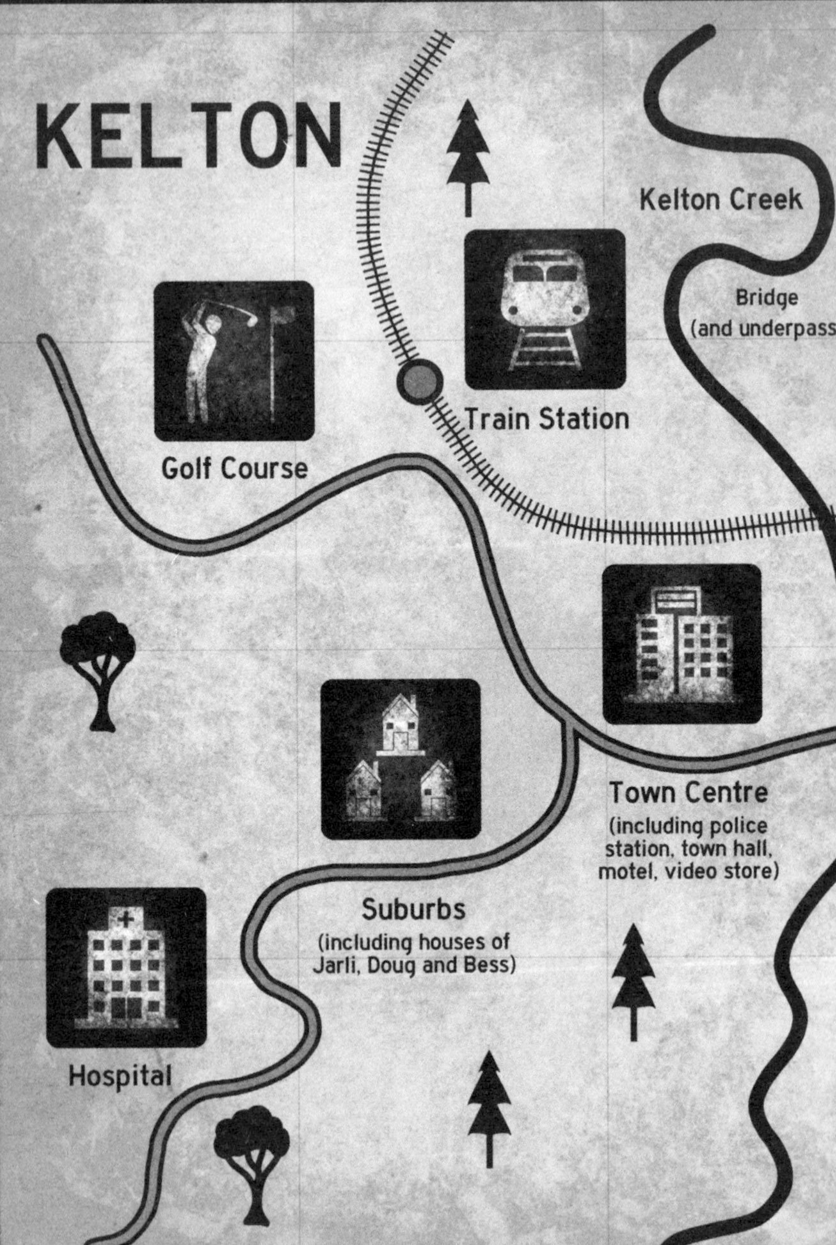
KELTON
Kelton Creek
Bridge
(and underpass)
Train Station
Golf Course
Town Centre
(including police
station, town hall,
motel, video store)
Suburbs
(including houses of
Jarli, Doug and Bess)
Hospital

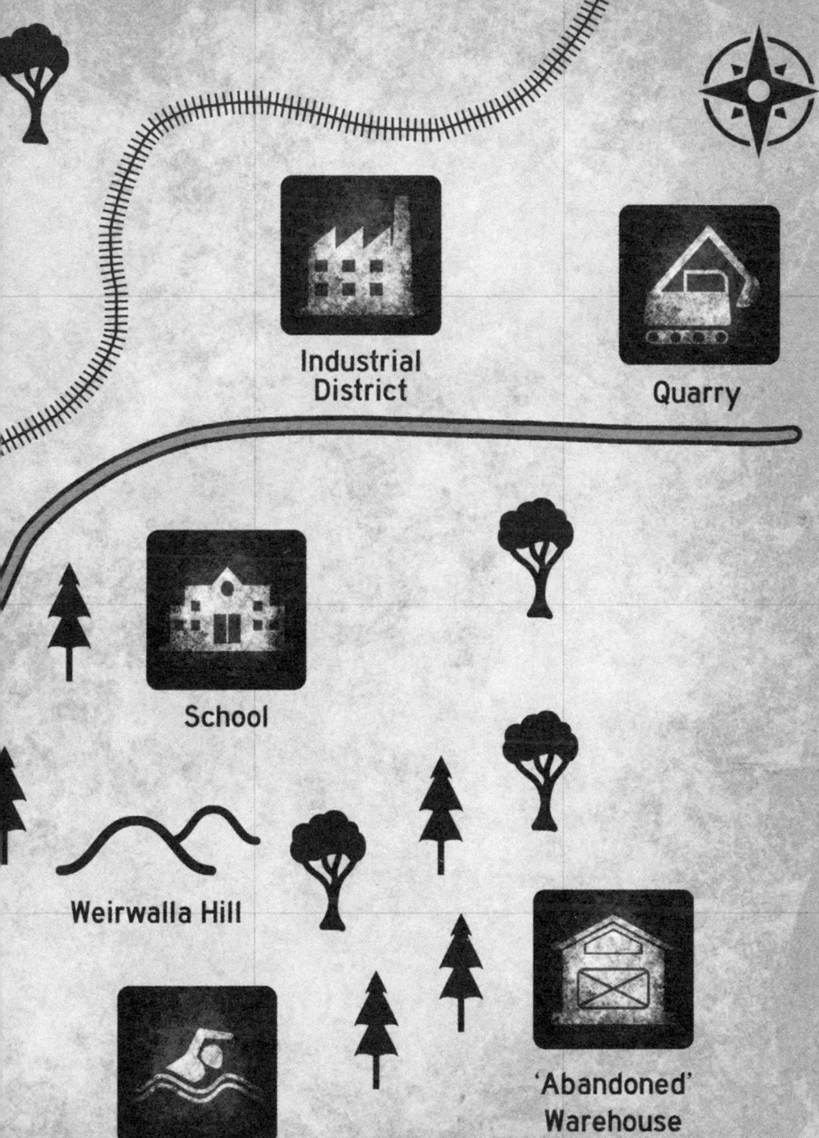
Industrial
District
Quarry
School
Weirwalla Hill
'Abandoned'
Warehouse
Lake

PART ONE: ULTIMATUM

OF COURSE, THE APP CAN ONLY TELL *IF* SOMEONE IS LYING. IT NEVER TELLS YOU *WHY*.

—From the documentation for Truth, *version 5.1*

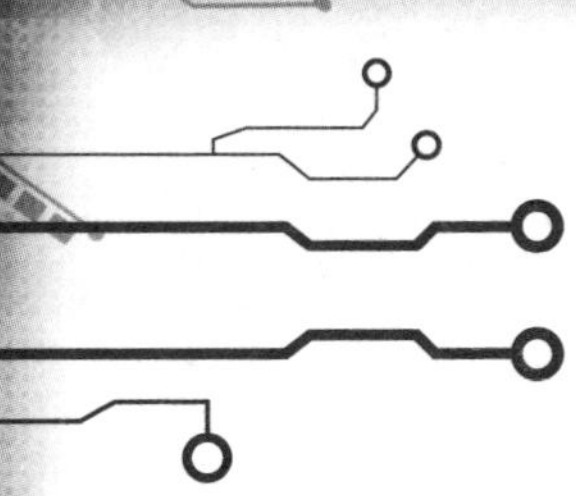

JAILBREAK

The slot opened. The masked face of a guard appeared in the gap.

'Move away from the door,' she said, her voice distorted by her breathing apparatus.

Doug obeyed, pressing his back against the concrete wall of his prison cell.

The lock clunked and the hinges groaned. The guard entered carrying a tray. Doug couldn't tell if she was the same guard who always came. She was covered head-to-toe in white plastic.

'What day is it?' Doug asked.

He tried a different question every time. *Where am I? Who are you? When can I go home? Do my parents know I'm alive?* As always, she didn't respond. But he knew she could hear him, because last time his question had been, *Could I have a book? And some reading glasses?* Now here they were on the tray, next to a bottle of water and a bowl of brown rice. No spoon.

Doug hadn't really expected the guard to give him

what he wanted. She worked for Viper, a criminal mastermind who stole weapons, poisoned people and once even crashed a plane. Doug still wasn't sure why Viper was keeping him alive.

And Doug wasn't the only one. He had heard other voices echoing around the prison. Someone sobbing, someone else screaming, somebody who wouldn't stop mumbling to themselves. Viper was holding a lot of people in here. The question was: why?

'Thank you,' Doug said.

The guard put the tray on the floor and backed out of the room without saying anything. The door slammed. The lock clunked. The slot closed.

Doug picked up the tray and sat down on the bed. The metal frame was hard beneath the thin foam mattress. The book was a dusty old horror novel, with a skeleton on the cover wearing a top hat. Doug ignored it, and picked up the reading glasses.

Yes, he thought. *These might work.*

Doug glanced at the door to check that the slot was still closed. Then he ripped one arm off the glasses. He prodded the jagged end of the arm with his fingertip. Too sharp. He scraped it against the concrete floor for a while, shaping the metal into a flat blade, like the head of a screwdriver. Then he lifted the mattress, exposing the bedframe.

Holding his breath, he poked the broken arm into the head of a screw, and TWISTED. The screw was too tight. Doug scraped the blade on the floor some more, flattening it for a better fit. This time it worked. The screw rotated, just a tiny amount. *Careful,* Doug told himself. He kept twisting, and soon the leg of the bed was loose.

He felt like cheering. Two suffocating weeks in this grey room, with nothing but fear and brown rice for company. He didn't know anything about the outside world. He didn't even know if his friends had survived the attack on the hospital.

But he was getting out of here.

A SECOND OPINION

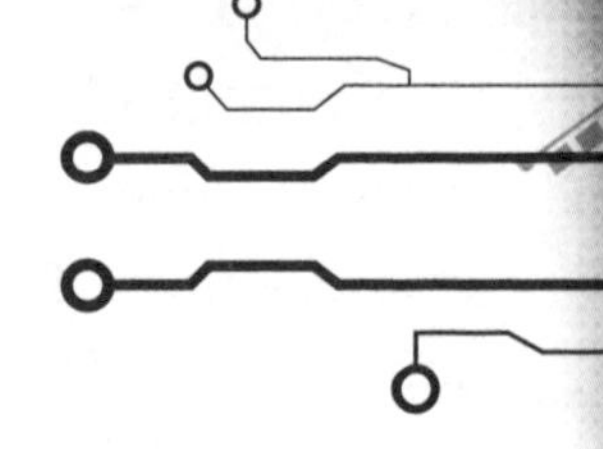

'Stop!' Plowman hissed. He dragged Jarli back behind the tree.

'What?' Jarli looked around at the deserted street. It was another quiet afternoon in Kelton, the sun beginning to dip below the horizon.

'A drone.' Plowman was staring at the darkening sky.

Jarli peered up through the branches of the tree. He could see a plane—Kelton lay under a major flight path—but no drones.

Listening, he could only hear the rustling of the leaves and the buzzing of insects.

'Where?' he asked.

'It's too high up to see.'

'How do you know it's there?'

'Look.' Plowman's arm was still in a sling, so it took him a while to get his phone out of his pocket. On the screen was a map of Kelton, covered with a vortex of spiralling dots. 'Those are drones. I get a notification when one is nearby.' He pointed. 'That one is passing over us right now.'

'Whose drone is it?'

'Mine.'

Jarli frowned. 'You're still spying on the town? I thought—'

'No-one is safe until Viper is caught,' Plowman said.

'But if it's your drone, why do you care if it sees us?'

'Because I still don't know how Viper's goons found me, before they dumped me in that car crusher. It's possible that Viper got into my network somehow.'

'So you built this surveillance system, and now you've lost control of it.' Anger flared in Jarli's chest. 'You're *helping* Viper spy on us.'

Plowman was looking at the dots on the screen again. 'OK, we're clear. Go, before another one comes!'

Jarli raced across the street to the apartment building, Plowman limping after him. All the windows were dark except one.

'I hope she's not freaked out to have one of her students visit her on the weekend,' Jarli said.

Kellin Plowman hesitated, his hairy finger hovering over the doorbell. 'Wait. She's the nurse from your school?'

Jarli reddened. 'Miss Eaton isn't just a school nurse,' he said. 'She used to be an army surgeon.'

'That might be useful if I had been shot,' Plowman said. 'But I've had my memories stolen instead. So unless she has experience treating memory theft on the battlefield—'

'I trust her.'

'You're not the one whose head she's supposed to examine.'

Well, it's not just you who had something taken. Jarli swallowed the words and fought the urge to touch the scab under his hair. After two weeks, the wound still itched. Jarli hadn't told Plowman or anyone else that Viper had stolen some of his memories, too. He had hoped the missing day would resurface somehow. But there was nothing—he had gone to bed on a Wednesday and woken up on a Friday, with only a grey gap in between.

'I don't think we should trust anybody,' Plowman said.

Funny, Jarli thought. Eaton had once told him the same thing.

The wind picked up, and the trees rustled in the street. A crow picked at some discarded chips in the gutter. Storm clouds gathered on the horizon.

'Eaton saved me from Viper several times,' Jarli said. 'So unless you want to go to a hospital—'

'No hospitals,' Plowman said automatically, as Jarli had known he would. The last time Plowman visited a hospital, it had been taken over by mercenaries who worked for Viper. They had stolen a biological weapon and killed one of Jarli's friends.

Poor Doug. Jarli swallowed. Doug's body had burned away to nothing. At the funeral, his parents had put flowers on an empty coffin. Doug had been working on designs for a new robot. He had been applying for early entrance to universities out of town. Now he would never do anything ever again.

Jarli shook off the gloomy thoughts. 'This is the only other place in Kelton where you'll find a second medical opinion,' he said. 'Unless you want to try a dentist? Or a vet?'

Plowman grimaced.

'So ring the doorbell already,' Jarli said. 'I'm freezing.'

This was true, but it wasn't the only reason he wanted to get inside. Being alone with Plowman was making him nervous.

In many ways, Plowman was the opposite of Jarli. He had invented a new kind of encryption which helped people keep secrets. Jarli had made a lie-detector app which exposed them. Plowman's creation had made him a billionaire, while Jarli had released his app for free and earned nothing.

Plowman had become a recluse up in the hills—most people didn't even know what he looked like. Jarli had become an unwilling international celebrity . . . and a target.

Plowman had said he didn't know who Viper was, and Jarli's app indicated that he was telling the truth. But the billionaire was also monitoring the whole town with his DRONES. Jarli got the feeling he wasn't entirely on the level.

Finally Plowman pushed the button. A buzzer echoed from somewhere inside the apartment building.

Jarli turned to the camera so Eaton would be able to see his face.

A voice crackled in the speaker. 'Jarli? What are you doing here?'

'Hi, Miss Eaton,' Jarli said. 'We need to talk to you.'

' . . . Well, OK. Come on up.'

There was another buzzer, and the gate clicked.

Eaton's apartment was small, clean and full of cardboard boxes, like she was just moving in. But that couldn't be right. Bess and Doug had visited her here months ago.

Jarli thought, *I should ask Doug if . . .* And then he remembered, again, that Doug was gone.

Plowman extended a hand. 'Kellin Plowman,' he said.

'We've met before.' Eaton looked him up and down, taking in the sling and the bruising on his face.

'We have?' Plowman looked confused.

'You helped me with a technology problem. You don't remember?'

'No. So that means . . .' Plowman turned to Jarli. 'Whatever happened, whatever Viper wanted to remove, it must have happened at around the same time. Maybe even the same day.' He turned back to Eaton. 'When was this?'

'Whoa, back up,' Eaton said. 'Did you say Viper is behind this visit?'

It took Jarli a few minutes to explain. Plowman had left a voicemail for Jarli, saying he knew Viper's identity and that they needed to meet up. The next day, Plowman had been kidnapped by Viper's mercenaries, who used a surgical laser to remove some of Plowman's memories.

Privately, Jarli assumed that Plowman had met with him and revealed Viper's identity before the mercenaries got to him. So Viper had taken Jarli's memories, too.

Eaton listened, her eyes wide.

'I wish I'd seen it,' Plowman added. 'Surgical robots are truly fascinating.'

'You're lucky to be alive,' Eaton said. 'Even with a robot, it takes a lot of skill to perform brain surgery without killing the patient.'

Jarli was still looking around at the boxes. The closest ones had CHARITY scrawled on the side. 'Are you moving?'

'Leaving Kelton,' Eaton said. 'Viper is making it too dangerous to stay.'

Jarli's heart sank. Not just because he would miss her. If a war veteran like Eaton thought it was too dangerous to live here, what hope did he and his friends have?

'Where are you going?' he asked.

Eaton glanced at Plowman. 'No offence, but I'd rather not share that information.'

Plowman held up his hands. 'Fair enough.'

When Jarli invented *Truth*, his lie-detector app, he had imagined a world where everyone trusted each other. But after his app went viral, people seemed more suspicious of one another than ever. Even worse, Viper had released *Truth Premium*, his own version of the app. *Truth Premium* was much more popular than Jarli's app, but it had a secret white-list. It was programmed to always believe certain people, no matter what they said. Now no-one could be trusted.

'Can you help me get my memories back?' Plowman asked.

'I doubt it,' Eaton said. 'But I can take a look at your head. Take a seat.'

There seemed to be only one chair in the whole apartment. Plowman sat down. Eaton washed her hands at the sink, scrubbing all the way up to her elbows. Then she stood behind Plowman, parting his thin hair to see the scar.

'Have you experienced any dizziness?' she asked, palpating his skull. 'Fatigue?'

'No.'

'Personality changes?' Eaton looked at Jarli.

Jarli shook his head. 'He doesn't seem any different.'

'I've been a bit jumpy,' Plowman admitted. 'Paranoid.'

'That's a normal reaction to being attacked.' Eaton let go of his head. 'Your face is a mess, as I'm sure you know. But there's no discolouration of the skin around the incision, and the bones of your skull feel like they're knitting together well. Whoever did this to you, they've done it before.'

Jarli again resisted the urge to touch his own scar.

'You should still go to a hospital.' Eaton went to the sink and washed her hands again.

'What about getting Mr Plowman's memories back?' Jarli asked.

'As I said, it's very unlikely.'

'But not impossible?'

Eaton dried her hands on a tea towel.

'Please,' Plowman said. 'I've run out of other options.'

'The brain is a web,' Eaton said. 'With trillions of connections between billions of cells. Viper *could* have used the laser to fry the cells containing the relevant memories. But if the point was to erase your memory without killing you, it would have been safer to snip the connections around them instead.'

'So the memories could still be there,' Plowman said slowly, 'but I just can't get to them?'

'Right.'

'How does that help me?'

'It doesn't,' Eaton said. 'But if Viper missed one of the connections—and there would have been thousands to get through—then you could access the memories. If you could find the connection.'

'How do I do that?'

Eaton shrugged. 'Try something new. Go somewhere you've never been before. Try to learn a musical instrument, or a second language. Creating new connections in your brain is your best hope of stumbling across the old ones. Have you considered, I don't know . . . a holiday in Paris?'

Plowman looked tempted.

'We don't have time for that,' Jarli said. 'Viper has struck four times over the last year. And Cobra is still out there. We're in danger.'

Cobra was an old man who worked for Viper. He had tried to kill Jarli and his father. He had kidnapped Jarli's friend, Anya. Then he had vanished from a police cell, never to be seen again.

'Well, you figured out who Viper was once before,' Eaton said. 'It's possible you will again. But if you want my medical advice, it's this: leave Kelton.' She opened her kitchen cupboard and started wrapping bowls in newspaper and loading them into another box marked CHARITY. 'It's your best hope of staying alive.'

A SICKENING CRACK

Doug hefted the leg of the bed. It was carbon steel—lightweight but strong. Half a metre long. Not much of a weapon, especially since the guard had a stun gun. But that wasn't why Doug had removed it.

He listened at the door to his prison cell. It didn't sound like anyone was coming. He could wait until lights-out, when they expected him to be asleep—but there would be less activity in the building. Less noise to hide behind. And besides, he was going crazy in here.

At one end of the leg were two small wings which had been bolted to the bed frame. Doug wedged one wing under the door and pulled the leg back.

The leverage multiplied Doug's strength. The hinges were strong, but the steel leg was stronger. With a sickening crack, the hinges popped off the door frame, and the door leaned inwards, hanging precariously by the lock mechanism.

Doug jimmied the door further open and poked his head into the corridor. Concrete walls. No windows. No people either, but someone would have heard the noise. He had to get out of here, now.

Doug pulled the broken door back against the frame so it looked closed, then he ran up the corridor, taking the steel bed leg with him. His bare feet made soft slapping sounds against the floor. He passed several other locked doors just like his. No time to check if the cells were occupied. No way to free anybody if they were. Doug would send help as soon as he was out of here.

He turned left, and then right. He passed an open door leading to what looked like a control room—lots of screens, several keyboards, some swivel chairs. No people. He ran down some metal stairs towards what he hoped was the ground floor. Viper's prison was way bigger than he'd guessed.

Doug found a fire door on the bottom level, and was about to push it open when he heard voices on the other side.

'We can't just leave them here.'

'Those are Viper's orders.'

'But they'll starve.'

'Not our problem. And no, they won't. When the rocket launches, there will be . . .'

The voices were getting closer. Doug turned and ran back up the stairs. When he reached the second landing, he heard the fire door open just below. The guards were coming up the stairs.

Doug headed in the direction of his cell—but skidded to a stop. A SHADOW moved on the wall at the other end of the corridor. Someone was coming from that direction, too. Fear clutched Doug's heart. He was trapped!

There was only one place to hide: the control room. He ducked inside, slowly closed the door and locked it. The guards would have keys, but at least he would have a few seconds of warning before they came in.

Doug turned to the bank of glowing monitors. Lots of security feeds of concrete corridors. Most were empty, but guards in plastic suits were walking through a few. One monitor showed the street outside, which Doug didn't recognise from this angle. There was no map, and he couldn't see an exit on any of the screens.

He sat down on a swivel chair and tapped at one of the keyboards. A dark screen lit up, revealing a spreadsheet full of nonsense numbers. After some quick searching, Doug found the email client.

He hesitated. His plan was to email someone for help. But if the guards happened to check, they would see his email in the sent folder. Even if he deleted it they might find it in the trash. They would know who he had contacted, and what he had said.

Instead, he opened a web browser and logged into an encrypted messaging service called kGram. He'd used it before, and had some contacts saved.

secure encryption service

Jarli!
Viper's guards are holding me prisoner! I don't know where I am exactly—the drone flew me to a warehouse about half an hour away from the hospital, and later there was a 20 minute van ride to somewhere else. I'm in a big building with lots of concrete. There are other prisoners too. Please help!

Doug paused, wondering what other useful information he could include. At that moment, an alarm sounded. The lights in the ceiling flashed red. The guards must have realised that his cell was empty. It wouldn't take them long to find him.

A pre-recorded voice echoed through the corridors of the building:

WARNING. AUTOMATIC SECURITY SYSTEM DEPLOYED.
WARNING. AUTOMATIC SECURITY SYSTEM DEPLOYED.

Doug typed frantically:

secure encryption service

At the warehouse I saw surgical patients with their faces bandaged up. They were practicing accents. I think that's how Viper is making people disappear—he's giving them new faces and new identities.
We thought Viper was a man with burn scars all over his face. But maybe he can do surgery on himself, too? If so, he could be anyone. Even someone we know.

The door rattled. Someone was trying to get into the control room.

secure encryption service

I won't be able to contact you again.
Please find me!

Doug attached the spreadsheet of nonsense numbers to the message in case there were any clues in it. He was about to hit **SEND** when he remembered that kGram messenger ran on the *Supply Chain* encryption network, which was owned by Kellin Plowman. Doug had been warned not to trust anyone in Kelton. But Plowman had been injured by Viper's thieves, hadn't he? That was how he had ended up at the hospital. He was one of the good guys . . . right?

There was no time to choose another messaging service. Doug clicked SEND, and then shut down the computer. If the guards looked at the browser history, they might see kGram in the list, but they wouldn't be able to log in. They wouldn't know who he had contacted.

The door burst open behind him.

Doug swivelled around in the chair and put his hands up, surrendering.

Then he screamed.

The thing in the doorway was not a person. It was a four-legged robot, about the size of a large dog. Six eyes stared at Doug from behind glass lenses. Plates of gunmetal grey armour gleamed in the red lights of the control room. Instead of a mouth, a long spike protruded from the robot's face, like the proboscis of a mosquito.

This was the automatic security system.

Doug scrambled out of the chair and backed away into the corner. The robot scuttled towards him, joints clicking and whirring. He snatched up the steel bed leg and flung it at the robot's head.

Clang! The robot didn't even seem to notice. It levelled its mouth-spike at Doug, and a transparent red fluid squirted out the end. Doug raised his arms to protect his face. The fluid covered his hands and tingled on his skin, like a prawn cracker dissolving on the tongue. It smelled artificially sweet. Medical. Doug wiped his hands on his shirt, but the sticky stuff wouldn't come off. He was getting dizzy.

'Get away from me!' he shrieked. But the robot was already reaching for him with a mechanical claw. Doug felt like he was falling into a black hole, faster and faster, so fast that he was getting *stretched*. His hands and feet felt a long way from his head, on the ends of long, floppy limbs.

Poison, he thought.

An electrified needle extended from the robot's claw. When it touched him there was a crackling sound. Doug felt all his limbs go rigid as the voltage hit him. Then the whole world went dark.

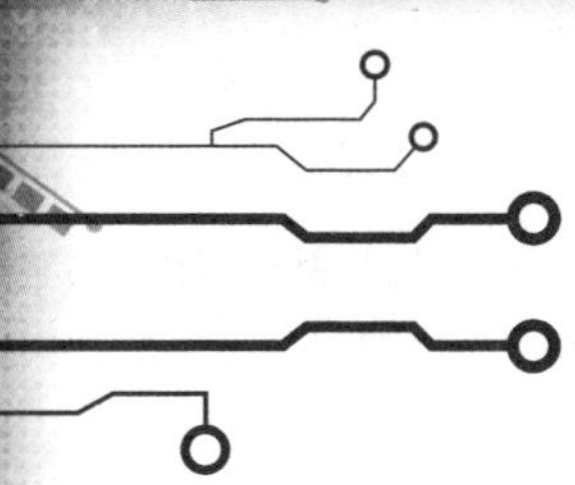

ENEMY WITHIN

'Where have you been?' Dad demanded.

Jarli paused on his way in the door. He wasn't late—he could smell dinner cooking in the kitchen.

'Out,' he said. 'With a friend.'

'Which friend?'

'Someone I met at the Robattle.' Jarli hoped this wouldn't set off his *Truth* app. He wasn't technically lying, but he did hope his father would think he was talking about a teenager. The app might pick up on his anxiety, or his intentionally vague phrasing.

He had intended to be completely honest with his parents about where he had been, and who he had been with. But something in Dad's tone made him think that wasn't a good idea.

'I am your father,' Dad snapped. 'I—'

'I'm aware,' Jarli said.

His new phone beeped. **LIE** The app wasn't supposed to react to sarcasm—maybe it wasn't interacting well with the updated operating system.

'I want to know where you are at all times,' Dad

said. 'Is that clear?'

Jarli hesitated. If he made a promise he knew he couldn't keep, the app would call him out on it.

'Why?' he asked instead.

Dad snatched the backpack out of Jarli's hands and headed for the kitchen.

'Hey!' Jarli tried to grab it back, but Dad held it out of reach. Most old people started to shrink, but if anything, Dad seemed to be getting taller.

He unzipped Jarli's backpack and started rummaging through it. Jarli was aghast. Dad had never acted like this before.

Dad pulled a tangle of charger cables out of the bag. 'What's this?'

'That's my stuff,' Jarli shouted. 'Give it back!'

Ignoring him, Dad dumped the cables on the kitchen floor and kept digging through the bag. He tossed out a comic book, a banana and a broken wheel from Doug's robot, which Jarli had been carrying around since Doug died. Jarli flinched as the wheel clattered against the floor tiles.

Next Dad pulled out an envelope. Jarli held his breath. He had already opened the letter—it was an offer for early admission to a university in the city. It was a great opportunity, but he needed to stay in Kelton to protect his friends and family from Viper. He hadn't told his parents about the offer in case they pressured him to take it.

Dad discarded the envelope and started leafing through Jarli's notebook instead, looking at the ideas that Jarli had sketched out for future versions of his app.

'What does all this mean?' Dad muttered to himself.

With that, Jarli's rage faded. Since the car crash, Dad had been having problems with his memory. Dr Vorham had told Mum that this was a normal reaction to trauma. Now Dad—a former IT professional—didn't even seem to recognise Python, the popular programming language Jarli had written his code in.

'I'm sorry, Dad,' Jarli said. 'I should have told you where I was going.'

Dad glared at him suspiciously.

Jarli gestured at the notebook. 'Those are just ideas for new features in my app,' he said. 'Do you want me to show you what they mean?'

'No.' Dad thrust the notebook back at Jarli.

Kirstie, Jarli's little sister, walked in. She went past the sizzling wok and opened the fridge without even glancing at Jarli or Dad. She had braided her hair and was wearing her favourite sparkly T-shirt.

'What are you two chuckleheads arguing about?' she asked, searching the fridge.

'Nothing,' Jarli and Dad both said at the same moment. Jarli's phone, Kirstie's phone and Dad's phone all beeped. LIE

Kirstie laughed and munched on a piece of parmesan. 'Good talk.' She turned to leave the room.

'Why are you all dressed up?' Dad asked suspiciously.

'I'm doing a video interview for an alien blog.'

Jarli groaned. His sister was obsessed with alien conspiracy theories, and she had a bad habit of dragging other people into them. 'You're not going to tell anyone you were abducted by aliens, are you?'

'Of course not.' Kirstie looked offended. 'I'm going to read the testimony of someone who was. The actual abductees can't go on camera in case the government tracks them down. There's a total conspiracy, you know.'

Normally Dad would try to talk Kirstie out of something like this. But today he just said, 'Whatever. Can you give Jarli and I some privacy?'

Kirstie looked disappointed. She loved riling Dad up, but today he hadn't taken the bait. 'OK. I'll be off then. Video chatting to *strangers* on the *internet*.'

When Dad didn't react to that, she huffed and stalked back to her room.

'Are we clear?' Dad said.

'Clear on what?' Jarli asked.

'From now on, you tell me exactly where you're going.' Dad was still holding the backpack out of reach, like a school bully. 'And who you're going with.'

Jarli sighed. 'Sure, Dad. I can do that.'

Dad handed him the bag. Jarli stuffed his things back inside, then escaped into his bedroom and closed the door. A minute later he heard Dad move away towards the lounge room.

Jarli sat on the bed and put his head in his hands. Dad's weirdness was only getting worse. And it seemed like there was nothing Jarli could do to fix it.

NO DEMANDS

When Detective Zee Arno looked through the peephole, she was horrified to see Dana Reynolds on her verandah. It was after dark, and the journalist had no camera crew, but she looked like she was here on business. Her glossy chestnut hair was sprayed to perfection, and she wore expensive, camera-ready clothes.

Arno unlocked the door and opened it a crack. 'How did you find out where I live?'

Reynolds smiled, revealing chemically-whitened teeth. 'I never reveal a source. Can I come in?'

Reynolds was supposed to be long gone. She had come to Kelton to interview that *Truth*-app kid, Jarli Durras. But she had stayed to investigate the shadowy criminal known as Viper—or so she said.

Detective Arno didn't like the media at the best of times. She especially didn't like it when they investigated the same cases as the police, contaminating evidence and interfering with witnesses. Worst of all were the journalists like

Reynolds, who always seemed to know way too much. It was almost suspicious, how quickly Reynolds showed up whenever Viper did anything.

'It's about Viper,' Reynolds added, as though she could read Arno's mind.

'Talk to me at the station,' Arno said. 'During business hours.' She started to close the door.

'It can't wait,' Reynolds said. 'Trust me, you'll be summoned to the station shortly anyway.'

Swallowing her dread, Arno unhooked the chain. 'Fine. Come in.'

Reynolds was tall, and wore heels—she had to lower her head to get through the front door of the old house. She looked around with shameless curiosity as soon as she was inside, taking in the photographs and medals on the walls. 'You were in the army?' she asked.

'Navy,' Arno corrected. 'Before I joined the police force.' She resisted the urge to offer Reynolds a tea or coffee. 'I thought you were investigating the defence minister?'

Reynolds waved a hand. 'I was. But I can't find any sources willing to go on the record about him. Anyway, a better story fell into my lap. Are you alone?'

'Yes,' Arno said uneasily.

'Good. I just received a message,' Reynolds said.

'From Viper.'

'What? What kind of message?' Arno was already on high alert.

'I'll show you.' Reynolds tapped her phone screen, and brought up a video. She hit **PLAY.**

The man on the screen wore a broad-brimmed black hat, so most of his face was in shadow, but hideous BURNS covered the rest of it. His eyes, unblinking, were sunk deep within the pink scar tissue. Behind him was a silver canister. The rest of the background was invisible in the darkness, but when he spoke, it sounded like he was in a small room.

'At noon tomorrow, the town of Kelton will become uninhabitable.' The man's voice was a distorted growl. The microphone hissed in the pauses between words. 'Everyone has until then to leave.'

Arno shot a glance at Reynolds. The journalist's face was unreadable.

'This is not a threat,' Viper continued. 'I have no demands. This is a statement of fact. Leave . . . or die.'

The video went dark.

Reynolds said, 'That canister in the background looks a lot like the vacuum flask stolen from the Kelton Research Hospital two weeks ago. The one that contained an untreatable strain of botulism H, a toxin created by the botulinum bacteria. My producer tells me that less than one millionth of a gram can be fatal. In short, Viper appears to possess a biological weapon capable of poisoning not only everyone in Kelton, but the entire human race. So . . .' She pulled a microphone out of her bag and pointed it at Arno. 'Would you care to comment?'

CELL MATES

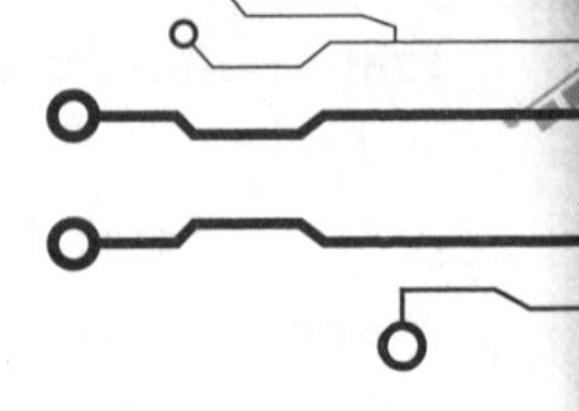

Doug woke up on the floor. When he tried to sit up, he was hit by a wave of nausea. He barely rolled over in time to vomit on the concrete.

Shaking, he wiped his chin and looked around. The guards had moved him to a different cell. Like his previous cell, it had concrete walls, but instead of a door, there were cage bars. A camera watched him from outside. He would have no privacy anymore. And this time there was no bed to disassemble. Just a mattress on the floor.

Even if Doug somehow escaped from his cell again, he didn't know how he'd get past the robot. Doug's hobby was designing small robots, submitting the designs for awards, and battling other bots in competitions. But he'd never seen anything as advanced as that terrifying mechanical guard.

Looking through the bars, Doug could see more cells on the other side of the corridor. All empty.

'Hello?' he called, not really expecting a reply.

His voice echoed, thin and weak.

'Hello,' someone said.

Doug jolted. The voice had come from quite close by. Maybe the cell next to his.

'Who's there?' he asked.

A cough. 'My name's Glen.'

Doug wished he had his phone, so Jarli's app would tell him whether that was true. 'I'm Doug,' he said. 'Are you a prisoner?'

'That's right. For three months and eight days now.'

'Is it just us here?'

'In this section, yes,' Glen said. 'I used to be somewhere else, where there were more people. They moved me here after I tried to escape.'

'Huh. Me too.'

'How old are you, Doug?'

'Sixteen,' Doug lied. It didn't feel safe to admit his real age.

There was no beep from the adjacent cell. Glen didn't have a phone either. 'Never mind,' he said. 'My son has a friend named Doug. I thought it might be you.'

'Where are we?' Doug asked.

'Have you heard of Throwaway?' Glen replied. 'It was on the news a while back, according to some of the other captives.'

Doug knew what Glen was talking about. The Minister for Defence, Aaron Fisher, had used a secret prison in Kelton—nicknamed Throwaway—to covertly detain kids who knew things that could embarrass the government. Doug, Jarli, Anya and Bess had exposed the truth, but the minister had blamed his deputy and managed to keep his job.

'I thought that place got closed down,' Doug said.

'Closed down, but not demolished. Now someone else is using it to make people disappear.'

Viper, Doug thought.

'I'm guessing that's where we are, anyway,' Glen continued. 'I don't think we've left Kelton, and where else in this town could you find a building like this?'

'And you've been here the whole time?'

'No. I was in a basement somewhere, first. Then this place, about six weeks ago.' Glen's voice broke. 'I . . . I miss my wife, and our children. I'm not even sure they know I'm alive. The guards won't tell me anything.'

Doug pushed his arm between the bars which made up the door. He reached for the neighbouring cell. After a moment, he felt a large, strong hand clutch his. It was unsettling, to hear such a big man so scared.

'Don't worry,' Doug said. 'We're going to get out of here. I managed to get out of my cell for a while.

Before they caught me, I sent a message to a friend. Help is coming.'

'Oh. That's good.' There was a note of forced optimism in Glen's voice.

'Your son,' Doug said. 'What's his name?'

'Jarli,' Glen said. 'My daughter is Kirstie.'

Doug snatched his hand back as though he'd been bitten by a snake.

'What?' Glen asked.

Doug's mind was racing. If this was Glen Durras, Jarli's dad, and he'd been captured more than three months ago . . .

Then who was the man living at Jarli's house?

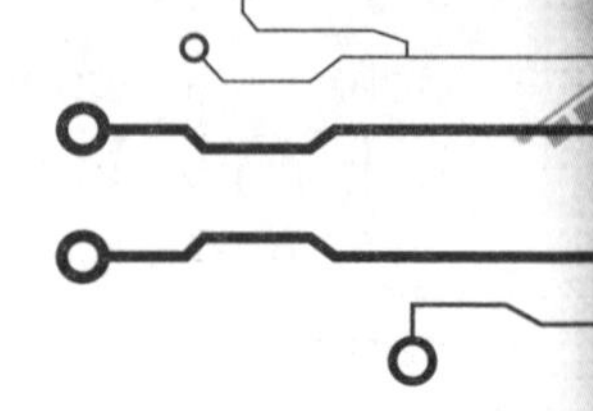

MASS PANIC

Jarli's phone dinged. A message from Bess:

> Jarli!!! Have you seen this?!

> State of emergency declared in Kelton
> *News Online*

> I'm scared.

Bess had been Jarli's best friend since they were little. She was a punky girl with a love of classic novels, a hatred of sport and a knack for charming strangers into doing whatever she wanted. She had been gloomy since Doug's death—she blamed herself—but Jarli had never heard her admit she was afraid. If Bess was scared, then Jarli was, too.

He sat down on his bed and tapped the link. A man with a black hat and a scarred face appeared on his phone screen.

'AT NOON TOMORROW, THE TOWN OF KELTON WILL BECOME UNINHABITABLE. EVERYONE HAS UNTIL THEN TO LEAVE. THIS IS NOT A THREAT. I HAVE NO DEMANDS. THIS IS A STATEMENT OF FACT. LEAVE . . . OR DIE.'

By the time the video was over, Jarli felt sick. He realised he was trembling. He'd witnessed the damage Viper's plans had done to the town. He'd heard his distorted voice. Both Eaton and Scanner—an undercover cop in Viper's organisation—had mentioned rumours about his appearance. But he'd never actually seen Viper. Seeing his face made it real.

Jarli did a quick web search. Maybe someone had already proven the video was a hoax.

Nope. Dana Reynolds had been the first to upload the video, and she was never wrong when it came to Viper. Since then, other news outlets had picked up the story. The headlines got worse and worse:

Criminal mastermind delivers ultimatum
Daily News

MAYOR SHELBY CALLS FOR CALM AMID KELTON CRISIS
SUN TELEGRAPH

As Jarli watched, another headline popped up.

Kelton to be evacuated after 'credible threat' ***Evening Bulletin***

On social media, hysterical posts and comments were multiplying.

QS **Quinn**

Viper WANTS us to evacuate. It's a trap. I bet he's put landmines on the roads out of town . . .

YR **Yasmin**

I left Kelton ages ago, right after that plane crash. Anyone still there must have a death wish.

OA **Oscar**

Leaving Kelton won't save anybody from Viper. I'm going into my basement with a year's supply of bottled water and canned food.

LW **Laura**

You actually think this 'Viper' is a real person? No way. The government wants to clear the land for something, like more of those nuclear tests . . .

AA **Ashley**

Good time to be a burglar in Kelton! Lots of empty houses.

Jarli's phone buzzed in his hand, and he jumped. Bess was calling.

He answered. 'Bess. I just watched the video.'

'So you're leaving, right?' Bess sounded out of breath. 'Me and Mum have almost finished packing the car. We'll be gone in an hour. But you'll be right behind us, won't you?'

'Um, hang on.' Jarli was still trying to wrap his brain around the initial threat. He checked his smart-watch.

'A lot could happen between now and noon tomorrow,' he said hopefully. 'The police could catch Viper, or the whole thing could turn out to be a hoax. Are you sure you want to leave right now?'

'Jarli. Listen to me.' Bess's voice was urgent. 'There are only two roads out of Kelton. Over the next fourteen hours, a thousand panicked people are going to try to take all their stuff out of town on those roads. It would only take two traffic accidents to trap everyone here. We have to get out before it's too late. Please, *please* tell me you're coming.'

'OK, OK,' Jarli said. 'Let me tell Mum and Dad what's going on.'

He walked into the kitchen to find them already arguing.

'I've lived here my whole life,' Mum was saying, tears in her eyes. '*Your* family has been here since before it was even a town. Now you're telling me you want to leave?'

Dad's face darkened with frustration. 'Do you know what "uninhabitable" means?' he demanded. 'If you stay here, you and your children—'

'Me and my children? What about *us* and *our* children? What has happened to you?'

Hooper was barking, excited by the raised voices. Kirstie was in the lounge room, looking from Mum to Dad and back again, her eyes wide.

Dad saw Jarli in the doorway. 'Jarli, get in the car,' he said. 'We're leaving.'

'Where are we going?' Jarli asked.

'I booked a hotel in Axe Falls,' Dad said. 'Grab a change of clothes. Nothing else.'

'You booked a hotel already?' Mum demanded. 'How?'

'You really want to fight about that now?'

Dad never spoke to Mum like this. *He's losing his mind,* Jarli thought. It was true that they needed to get out of town, but Dad was freaking Mum and Kirstie out.

'I'll ride with Dad,' Jarli said, hoping to defuse the situation. Luckily, they had bought a second car when Dad got his new job. 'Mum, you can take Kirstie in the other car. That way we can take more of our stuff.'

'Jarli . . .' Mum looked betrayed.

'We have to go, Mum. I'm sorry.' Jarli hugged her, like Dad should have done. Like he had done in every previous crisis. Mum squeezed Jarli tightly.

'This is our home.' There were tears in her eyes.

'I know. I love living here.' Jarli's own eyes were stinging. 'But I don't love the idea of dying here. Hopefully this will turn out to be nothing, and we can come back. OK?'

Mum finally nodded. 'OK.'

Jarli waited for Dad to apologise for losing his temper. He didn't.

'Grab some clothes,' Dad said. 'All of you.'

'And anything else that will fit in the cars.' Jarli met Dad's gaze. 'It will only take an extra minute.'

Dad gritted his teeth, but nodded. 'Fine.'

KNOWING TOO MUCH

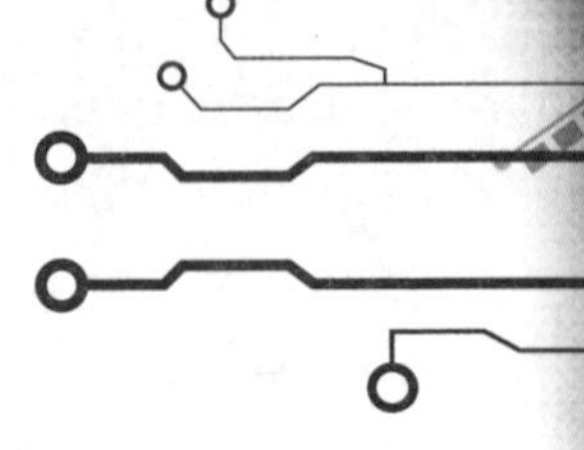

Reynolds picked up on the second ring. 'Detective,' she said. 'Do you have a statement for me yet?'

Arno gritted her teeth. 'I told you not to post that video.'

'And I told you that the public has a right to know that they've been threatened.'

Arno swung the steering wheel. She was on her way to Kelton police station, but it was taking forever. The roads were already clogged by frightened people, their back seats piled high with all their possessions.

'Don't get self-righteous with me,' Arno spat. 'You don't care about the public. You were just afraid that some other vulture would get the scoop. So you did exactly what Viper wanted, and created a frenzy.'

'You've misjudged me, Detective,' Reynolds said, and she sounded sincere—just like she did on the TV every night. 'I absolutely care about the public. But it's true that Viper almost certainly sent his video to other journalists. How long did you think you could keep this under wraps?'

Finally Arno pulled into the police station. A crowd of desperate, angry people blocked the front door. Civilians trying to get in, cops holding them back. Maybe they thought they would be safe in there.

Arno wished that were true. But the building wasn't airtight, and from the short briefing about BOTULISM H, she knew that a particle smaller than a speck of dust could kill. It paralysed the body bit by bit, weakening the muscles until they couldn't move at all. When it reached the lungs, the victim suffocated.

The canister containing botulism H had been at the Kelton Research Hospital because the doctors were trying to synthesize an antitoxin. They hadn't succeeded. Then Viper's mercenaries had stolen it.

Arno grabbed her phone and clambered out of the car. 'Thanks to you,' she told Reynolds, 'the public knew before the mayor did, which gave us no time to plan the evacuation of the town. If anyone gets hurt in the panic—and they will—it's on you.'

'Can I quote you on that?' Reynolds asked. '"Senior detective threatens journalist" would make a great lead story for my next broadcast.'

The detective ignored this. Something Reynolds

had said a minute ago had caught up to her. *Viper almost certainly sent his video to other journalists.* His *video*.

'In the recording, Viper's voice was distorted,' Arno said, thinking aloud. 'Run through some kind of filter.'

'Obviously,' Reynolds replied.

'I didn't pay much attention, because his voice has always been distorted. But this time we could see his face. Why bother disguising his voice if he was revealing his face?'

She could almost hear Reynolds shrugging on the other end of the phone. 'Habit, maybe?'

Arno pushed through the crowd towards the door. 'I doubt that. Everything Viper does, he does deliberately. I think he was wearing a mask.'

'It didn't look like a mask.'

No, Arno thought, *but someone like Viper would have the means and connections to obtain a convincing, realistic mask*. Besides, if a man with scars like that lived in Kelton, she would have noticed him. By supposedly revealing his face, Viper had stopped everyone from wondering what he looked like, and had made himself more invisible than ever.

'We don't know anything about him,' Arno realised.

'We know the threat is real,' Reynolds said. 'I ran

Truth Premium over the recording. So did a million other viewers. He's telling the truth about making Kelton uninhabitable.'

Arno wrenched the door of the police station open. She remembered a conversation she'd had months ago with Jarli Durras, the kid who had invented the original *Truth* app. He'd had a theory that *Truth Premium* had a white-list. It was programmed to trust certain voices, no matter what they said.

'*Truth Premium* is compromised,' she said.

'What do you mean?'

'It makes some people appear as though they never lie.'

Reynolds didn't reply.

'I can see why *you* wouldn't want to believe the app was flawed,' Arno continued. 'What's your honesty rating, again? A hundred per cent, right?'

More silence. It was possible that Reynolds had bought her way onto the white-list, so the app always trusted her. Or maybe she was always completely honest. She was either very good, or very bad.

In fact, Arno realised, no-one had never proven Viper was male. Everything they knew about him came from rumours.

'What are you implying?' Reynolds asked coldly.

'I'm not implying anything,' Arno said. 'Do me a

favour—don't leave town. I'm sure you want to stay here anyway, to report on the evacuation. For the benefit of the public.'

She ended the call and grabbed the nearest police officer—a young man with tanned skin and a thin moustache. 'Hey, you.'

The young man bristled. 'We've met. My name is Terry.'

'Good for you. I need you to put a trace on Dana Reynolds's phone.'

'Are you joking?' Terry demanded. 'We have half the people in Kelton jamming up the roads and the other half trying to get into this building. At the same time, we're searching the whole town for a biological weapon and a terrorist. You want me to take a break from managing all that so I can bug a journalist?'

'Yes,' Arno said. 'I think it's possible that journalist is Viper.'

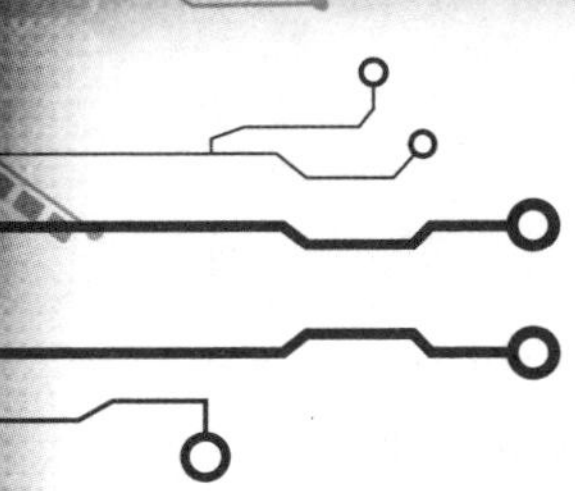

DAD?

'You're scaring Mum and Kirstie,' Jarli said.

Dad kept his eyes on the road, squinting against the reflected glare of the headlights. His knuckles were tight around the steering wheel. The sight reminded Jarli of something, but he wasn't quite sure what.

'They should be scared,' Dad said.

'Not of you. We're all supposed to look out for each other.'

Dad just grunted.

'I know you're afraid, too,' Jarli said. 'And I know it's been hard, since the crash. But you've gotta try to—'

'Shut up and let me focus on driving,' Dad said. Which was ridiculous. They were stuck in a traffic jam. Like Bess had said, there were only two roads out of Kelton, and both were full. Exhaust fumes pooled under a seemingly endless line of cars. The trees on either side of the road were lit by a blood-red glow of brake lights.

Over the last hour, the suburbs had turned into a warzone. A mixture of police, army and emergency services people had been driving through the streets with lights flashing and sirens screaming. Some were knocking on doors while others shouted into megaphones: 'Evacuate the town. Take your loved ones. Leave your belongings behind. This is not a drill. Evacuate the town. Take your loved ones . . .'

Despite all this, Jarli couldn't staunch the worry that some people would be left behind. Heavy sleepers. People who were hard of hearing, or didn't speak English. People with mobility issues, like Bess.

Jarli turned his face to the window. There was no getting through to Dad. When they got to the hotel, maybe Jarli could contact Dr Vorham somehow. Let him know that Dad's mental state was getting worse.

Mum and Kirstie had left five minutes before Jarli and Dad did. Jarli couldn't see their car ahead—maybe they had gotten out of town before the traffic slowed to a crawl. He checked his phone. No messages.

Ding! A notification from kGram appeared. Battery-saver mode was switched on, so mobile data only downloaded when the phone was unlocked.

Jarli frowned. He hadn't used kGram in weeks. Not since Doug died—no-one else he knew had an account.

He opened the message.

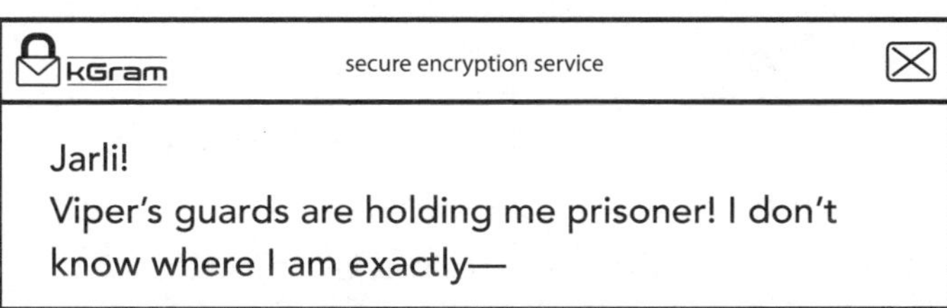

Jarli's eyes grew wider and wider as he read the message. Was this a sick joke? Had someone hacked Doug's account?

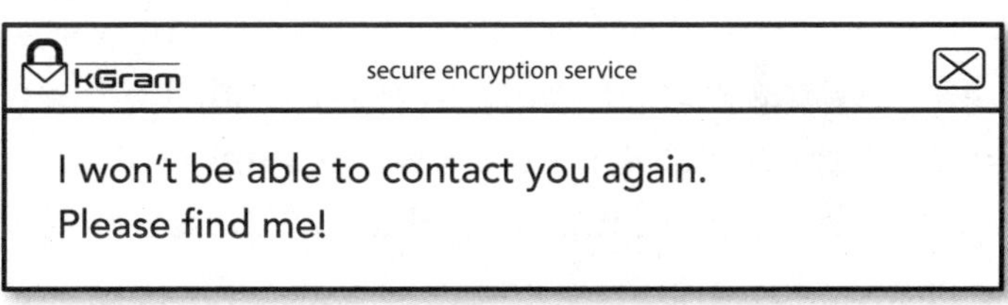

Doug had used long pass-phrases to protect his accounts, and his username was *MajorGriff*. Nothing like his real name. A hacker wouldn't have enough information to fake a message like this.

It was real. Doug was alive!

'Stop the car!' Jarli cried.

'The car *is* stopped,' Dad said.

'I just got a message from Doug.' Jarli brandished the phone. 'He's alive! Viper is holding him captive!'

Dad didn't look surprised. 'Your friend is dead. You were at his funeral.'

Jarli stared at him. What was Dad talking about?

The funeral didn't prove anything. The COFFIN had been empty.

Beep. LIE There must be a bug in the latest version of Jarli's code, since what Dad had said was true. Jarli *had* been at the funeral.

Dad swore. 'Will you turn that thing off?'

'You don't understand.' Jarli was already forwarding Doug's message to Bess and Anya. 'Doug is being held captive. He needs our help.'

'No, *you* don't understand.' Dad honked the horn at the driver in front of him, as though they could somehow get out of the way. 'We'll all be dead if we don't get out of here by noon tomorrow. Even if your friend is somehow still alive, there's nothing we can do for him.'

Jarli's phone dinged again. A message from Anya.

Where are you?

The western highway out of town. Trying to get my Dad to turn around. Are you still in Kelton?

'We can't just leave him to die,' Jarli said, typing as he talked.

'That's exactly what we're going to do,' Dad snapped.

Jarli opened his mouth and closed it again. Being forgetful and rude was one thing. But when had his father become so heartless?

'I'm going to call the police,' Jarli said.

Dad looked sharply at him. 'Why?'

'What do you mean, why?! To tell them to rescue Doug!'

Dad snatched the phone out of Jarli's hands. 'No. I told you to turn that off.'

Jarli was furious. 'And I told you Doug needs help!'

Dad stuffed the phone in the right-hand pocket of his jeans, where Jarli couldn't reach it. The phone didn't seem to fit, so he took out some leather gloves to make room.

Jarli stared at the gloves in Dad's lap. Cobra, the old man who had rammed Dad's car a year ago, had worn leather gloves just like those. Jarli had seen his emotionless face moments before impact, and his gloved hands gripping the steering wheel of the brown ute. The image was burned forever into Jarli's mind.

'Where did you get those?' Jarli asked.

'Get what?' The traffic started moving again, a painful crawl up the highway.

'The gloves.'

Dad said nothing. He braked as the traffic ahead

slowed to a stop once more.

Jarli felt like he was trapped in a falling lift. He thought of all the things 'Dad' seemed to have forgotten. His changing personality. The way his face still didn't look right, more than a year after the crash.

Part of Doug's message flashed through his brain: *That's how Viper is making people disappear—he's giving them new faces and new identities.*

'Never mind,' Jarli said. His mouth was suddenly dry. Unless he was losing his mind—and that was what it felt like—he was trapped in this car with Cobra. Someone who had once tried to murder him.

And Dad—his real Dad—was missing.

'I feel sick,' Jarli said, unbuckling his seatbelt and opening the passenger door. His phone didn't beep in Cobra's pocket, because this was true. But as soon as Jarli's feet hit the ground he was running, off the highway and down the grassy slope into the darkness of the bush.

'Hey!' Cobra yelled. 'Get back here!'

Jarli heard the other door open, but he didn't dare look back. He reached the trees and kept running, pushing branches aside and trampling leaf litter. Maybe he should have run back along the highway instead, calling out to the other drivers. No-one would have believed him—*Help! A killer stole my*

Dad's face!—but Cobra might not have attacked him in front of witnesses. Too late now.

Jarli ran deeper and deeper into the bush. Looking back, he couldn't see the road anymore. But he could hear Cobra crashing through the undergrowth somewhere in the darkness. Jarli took an abrupt left turn, ducked under a thick bough and crawled into a gloomy hollow between two trees, out of sight. He stayed perfectly still, knees and fingertips on the dirt, heart racing.

'Get back here, kid,' Cobra yelled. Dad never called him 'kid'. Where was Dad?

The footsteps drew closer. Jarli trembled in his hiding place. If Cobra found him, there was nothing he could do. He should have stayed on the road. Or even in the car—pretended he didn't know the truth.

The footsteps stopped. Jarli clenched his teeth so hard they hurt. Had Cobra spotted him? Or was he listening, because he'd lost the trail?

Ding! It was Jarli's phone, in Cobra's pocket. He was standing right next to the bough which concealed Jarli's hiding place.

Cobra pulled the phone out of his pocket. 'I know you're there, son,' he shouted. 'I'm sorry I took your phone. Come out and you'll be safe. I promise.'

The phone beeped. **LIE**

Cobra cursed, threw it on the ground and stomped on it.

Then Jarli heard something else. Footsteps, further away. Someone was hiking through the bush towards them.

A torch flitted between the trees. Jarli heard Cobra duck down, trying to get out of sight.

Too slow. The torch beam swung around towards him. 'There! I see him!' called a voice. Male . . . and somehow familiar to Jarli.

Cobra turned and bolted. The torchlight flickered as his pursuers ran closer and closer.

'Don't let him get away! If he tells Viper what he knows—'

'On it.' The second voice was younger, and female. Also familiar.

Jarli stood up. 'He went that way!' He pointed with one hand, shielding his eyes with the other.

The man lowered the torch. 'Jarli. Are you hurt?'

'No.' Jarli looked around, but couldn't see the young woman.

'It's Cobra, right? Is he alone?'

Jarli recognised the man now. He had a square nose, curly brown hair and dark circles around his eyes. Jarli didn't know his real name, but in his head he called him Scanner. He was—or had claimed to be—a police officer, undercover in Viper's gang.

'He's alone,' Jarli said. 'He's disguised as my dad.'

'Glen Durras. I know. Follow me.' Scanner ran past Jarli into the thick scrub, and disappeared.

Jarli scooped up his phone. It had a waterproof, shock-resistant cover which would survive an asteroid impact. Cobra's foot didn't appear to have damaged it.

Jarli wove through the trees after Scanner, branches snagging the threads on his shirt. He couldn't see Scanner anymore, but he could follow the sound of the footsteps in the undergrowth. As he stepped around a thick tree, he came face to face with—

'Anya?' he said, stunned.

Anya covered her torch and looked him up and down. 'Hello, Jarli. I am glad to see that you are OK.'

'How . . . what are you doing here?' Jarli asked.

'I got your message,' Anya said. 'We came as fast as we could.'

Scanner emerged from the trees behind her. 'Anything?'

'Sorry, Dad,' Anya said. 'I lost him.'

Jarli boggled at her. *'Dad?'*

Scanner and Anya looked at each other.

'There are some things I have not told you,' Anya said.

THE FAIL SAFE

'Excuse me, Minister.'

Aaron Fisher looked up from his prawn linguini. 'I'm eating dinner,' he said. *Was an hour's peace and quiet too much to ask?*

The assistant minister for defence, Sandra Rizvi, hovered in the doorway. 'We need to talk about a contingency plan,' she said. 'In case that biological weapon is released in Kelton.'

Fisher dabbed at his mouth with a napkin. 'I thought that was taken care of.'

'We've dispatched hundreds of troops to search for the weapon,' Rizvi said. 'But there's no guarantee that they'll find it. Even if they do, they may not be able to defuse it.'

She sat down in the plush chair opposite Fisher, who sighed with annoyance. His dinner was going cold.

'So what?' he said. 'Haven't we evacuated the town anyway?'

Rizvi looked worried. 'We're trying, but even in

a well-planned evacuation—which this isn't—there are some people who cannot or will not leave. And all our troops are obviously in the danger zone.'

Fisher looked out the window over the sparkling lights of the city. He had a flight tomorrow. He should be packing right now.

'That's their job,' he said. 'To be in dangerous places.'

'We still have a responsibility for their safety,' Rizvi said.

The words triggered something. That journalist, Dana Reynolds, had been hassling him again about Malburse. Every time he thought that whole mess was behind him, it found a way to rise back to the surface.

He had quashed the story, for now. But if more soldiers died, and he got the blame, someone might talk.

'Pull the troops out of Kelton,' he said.

'What?'

'Pull them out. Like you said, we have a responsibility.'

'But then they won't find the weapon,' Rizvi said. 'The toxin could spread for hundreds of kilometres, making the area uninhabitable for decades—'

'Does fire kill it?'

'I'm sorry?'

'Fire,' Fisher said. 'If we hit Kelton with a fuel-air bomb, will the virus die?'

'It's, uh, not a virus—and I don't know.'

'Well, find out. And get the troops out of there, so it's an option.'

'But . . . what about all the people still in Kelton?' Rizvi demanded, aghast.

'They'll have to evacuate. After the blast, they can come back and rebuild—which they couldn't do with bioweapon particles hanging in the air. Fire is easier to recover from.'

'Some people *can't* evacuate,' Rizvi insisted. 'They don't have access to cars, or they have mobility problems, or they're hard of hearing and don't know the evacuation is happening—'

'I've done my job,' Fisher said. 'I've made a decision. Now you do yours. Make it happen. *Discreetly.*'

Rizvi looked ready to mount further objections. *Why are all my deputies so uppity?* Fisher wondered. *Can't get good help these days.*

'Do I need to remind you who's in charge here?' he asked. 'Or what happened to the last assistant minister?'

Rizvi lowered her eyes. 'No, sir.'

'Good. Schedule the launch for 11 a.m.' Fisher paused with a forkful of food halfway to his mouth.

'One more thing. Viper never said that he would use botulism—he only said he would make the town uninhabitable. So leak a story that he might have access to a fuel-air bomb. When it goes off, I don't want to get the blame.'

THE LONG CON

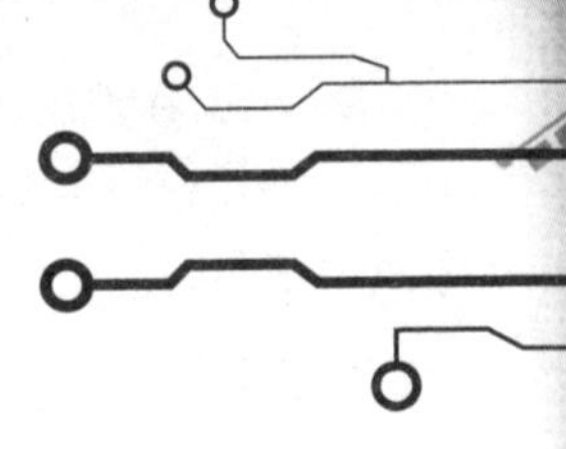

Anya and Scanner—he still hadn't told Jarli his real name—had abandoned their four-wheel drive on the shoulder of the highway half a kilometre away. The long trudge back to it, through the bush, out of sight of the road, gave Anya plenty of time to tell Jarli the whole story.

She and her family had been sent to Kelton as part of Operation Snake Basket—a secret police task force set up to catch Viper and dismantle his criminal empire. They had posed as a normal family for two years. A fake paper trail had been set up, making it look like Scanner had a criminal record and some bad debts. Eventually, that had been enough to lure Viper in.

'He sent a messenger with my first job,' Scanner said. 'A test. Viper told me to pick up some stolen cash from a warehouse on the southeast edge of town. Then he wanted me to break into someone's house and plant the cash there, framing him for a bank robbery.'

'So what did you do?' Jarli asked.

'Exactly what I was told,' Scanner said.

'But what about the guy who owned the house?'

'He went to jail. We'll get him released once Viper is caught.'

Anya wouldn't meet Jarli's eye.

'After that, I was in,' Scanner said. 'To prove my loyalty, I let Viper—that is, one of his doctors—put a radio-activated poison capsule in my hand. Then he started giving me bigger and bigger jobs. And I've been getting closer to his inner circle, while also passing on everything I know to the task force.'

The poison capsule would have sounded far-fetched if Jarli hadn't seen it with his own eyes. One of Viper's employees had died right in front of him, killed in seconds by a signal from a phone.

'The doctor,' Jarli said. 'Was it Doctor Vorham? A tall, thin guy with grey hair?'

'No, it was a woman. Why?'

'Doctor Vorham has been treating Dad. I thought he might have helped Viper make the swap.'

'Hmm,' Scanner said. 'If he's not involved, it's certainly suspicious that he didn't notice the change . . . although neither did you, of course.'

Jarli felt his cheeks redden. He changed the subject. 'If you're all from Russia, how come Anya and her mum have accents, but you don't?'

'I worked in counter-intelligence for years,' Scanner said, and suddenly his voice changed completely. 'I was trained in five languages and a dozen accents.'

'I am still learning,' Anya said. 'G'day, mate!'

Jarli winced. 'So where's my dad? And how did you know that Cobra had taken my father's place?'

'You know Throwaway?' Scanner asked. 'The old prison on Edward Street?'

Jarli shuddered. Yes, he knew it. He had been held captive there when the defence minister was still using it for juvenile detention.

'The police think it's sealed up and abandoned. But my task force just discovered that Viper has secretly taken it over. He's been using it as a base of operations for months.'

The trees thinned out, and the mud-spattered four-wheel drive appeared up ahead. Scanner unlocked the door, and they all climbed in. But the road was still blocked by the traffic jam, so they couldn't go anywhere.

'This morning Viper started getting all his people and equipment out of Throwaway,' Scanner was saying. 'Presumably because he's about to destroy the whole town. I was sent in to assist with the move. I helped the guards load a dozen prisoners into a transport truck. While I was there, I saw your father on one of the security monitors, in a cell. Later I established that his family hadn't reported him as missing. The only explanation was that he'd been replaced.'

It felt like a hand was squeezing Jarli's heart. 'Did my dad end up on the transport truck?'

'No. They were evacuating a different section.'

'Did he seem OK?'

'I didn't get a good look at him,' Scanner said.

Viper replaced my dad, Jarli thought, *and I didn't even notice*. The guilt was crushing. How long had his father not been his father?

'I bet that's the same place Doug is,' Jarli said. 'We have to go get them.'

Anya began, 'That's where we're—'

'No,' Scanner interrupted.

Anya looked confused. 'What do you mean? I thought—'

'The guards may be gone, but the prison has an automatic security system, and it's extremely dangerous. We don't have time to work out a way past it. In twelve hours Viper will turn this whole town into a graveyard.'

'Exactly.' Jarli drummed his fingers impatiently on his jeans. 'We have to get my Dad out of there—and Doug, too—before that happens!'

'*I* need to find and neutralise the canister of

botulism H.' The traffic shifted, and Scanner eased the vehicle forwards. 'That's the best chance of survival for your father, and for everyone else in Kelton.'

'We can't just leave them!'

Anya spoke up. 'We do not know where the canister is. Correct?'

Scanner nodded. 'I've ruled several places out, but there's still a huge search area. Without Cobra, we have no more leads. That's why we can't afford to waste any more time.'

Jarli realised that Scanner hadn't cared about him at all—he had only wanted to question Cobra about the toxin. Rescuing Jarli had been 'a waste of time'.

'Have you ruled out the prison?' Anya asked carefully.

'I see what you're saying,' Scanner said. 'But it's unlikely to be there. The building is airtight. If Viper released the botulism there, it wouldn't infect the rest of the town.'

'Unless Viper put it on the roof,' Anya pointed out. 'It would disperse well from up there.'

Jarli's mind was racing. 'And even if it's not in the building,' he said quickly, 'Dad could help you figure out where it is. He used to work for a company called CipherCrypt, and Viper was connected to it. Dad knows all sorts of things about Viper's organisation.'

'He shared that information with the police already,' Scanner said.

'You don't know what he's overheard or figured out since he got captured, though,' Jarli insisted. 'Doug, too. I last saw Doug at the same hospital that Viper stole the botulism from. He might know where it is.'

Scanner glanced in the rear-view mirror, thinking.

'Jarli makes a good point,' Anya said.

'He does,' Scanner said finally. 'But it's too dangerous. The security system includes an autonomous robot. It can't be bribed, threatened or reasoned with.'

'I bet it can be switched off, though,' Jarli said.

'Even if I knew how to do that—and I don't—we'd never get close enough. The thing will shoot us on sight.'

Jarli never wanted to see that prison again, especially not if it was guarded by a KILLER ROBOT. But he was going to rescue Dad and Doug, no matter what.

'I know someone who can help us,' he said.

THE WRONG MEMORIES

Kellin Plowman sat on a camping chair on the roof of his house, a flask of peppermint tea in one hand and a pair of binoculars in the other. From up here he could see all of Kelton. It looked like a disintegrating galaxy, the lights in the centre going dark one by one, red tail lights streaming outward as the people fled.

Plowman wasn't leaving. His house was at the top of a hill on the edge of town. However Viper was planning to disperse the botulism, it wouldn't reach him up here.

He squirted some more insect repellent on his upper arm and pulled his sling aside so he could rub it under the rim of the cast. The cold made his injuries ache. He wrapped the shawl more tightly around himself. It was past midnight, but he couldn't sleep. As a boy he had often sat on the roof of his parents' house, waiting for his father's car to turn the corner at the end of the street. Then he would race down the stairs to tell his mother, who would pretend to be excited. Sitting up here was bringing back memories, but not the ones he wanted.

Something was tugging at the edges of his mind, but it seemed to VANISH whenever he looked directly at it. The more he chased it, the further away it got, like a mirage. The tugs got stronger whenever he was tinkering with his robots, which seemed like a clue. Had one of his robots or drones led him to Viper's identity?

But the missing memories themselves never resurfaced. Viper had defeated him. And Kellin Plowman didn't suffer defeat lightly.

His phone rang, and he jolted in his seat. The camping chair wobbled, and nearly toppled off the roof. He shouldn't be up here. If he broke his other arm, life would be impossible. Cursing, Plowman found his phone and checked the screen. *Jeremy Dillon*. There was no such person—wary of getting hacked, Plowman always saved his contacts under aliases.

He answered. 'Jarli. Have you learned anything new about Viper?'

'Uh, not exactly.' Jarli sounded like he was in a vehicle. Evacuating, presumably. 'But we have a lead.'

Plowman shifted uneasily in his chair. 'Who is "we"?'

It took Jarli a few minutes to explain about Cobra, his father, Throwaway and the automated security system. Plowman didn't interrupt. When Jarli was finished, Plowman said, 'Tell me more about this robot.'

A new voice came on the phone. 'Fully autonomous, 360 degree scanning LIDAR, armed with an anaesthetic spray and a stun gun. It weighs eighty kilos, but the body is carbon fibre, so most of that weight is the battery. It can run for two days between recharges. Less if it has to stun somebody.'

There was that tugging again. A strange sense of familiarity.

'Who are you?' Plowman asked. Jarli hadn't told him who he was with.

The man didn't answer.

'OK,' Plowman said slowly. 'And this thing can move around?'

'Yeah. It has four legs. Sixteen joints in total. It can open doors, pick itself up if it gets knocked over—the works.'

'And how do you switch it off?'

'If I knew that, we wouldn't be calling you.'

Plowman thought about this. 'Well, it would make sense to have a remotely triggered shut-down feature,' he said, 'and a manual off-switch on the robot itself for backup.'

'Makes sense,' the man agreed. 'I don't have login details for Viper's network, so I can't access the controls for the robot. Viper uses your encryption, so Jarli was hoping you could help us hack it.'

'My encryption is unhackable,' Plowman said. 'Jarli should know that.'

'Then how did Viper get into your network?'

Plowman gritted his teeth, and winced—his jaw was still sore. 'I assume he got the password somehow,' he said.

There was some arguing at the other end of the line. Plowman climbed through the window, back into his house. He climbed down the stairs past piles of old books, wove through the boxes of mechanical junk in his living room, and entered the four-car garage through an internal door.

For a moment, he hesitated. To help Jarli, he'd have to leave his hilltop fortress. If he went back into the town, the toxin could kill him.

But if he *didn't* help Jarli, Viper would win. Plowman started shifting boxes around in the garage.

'We can wear hazard suits to protect us from the anaesthetic spray,' a young, female voice was saying.

'We don't have any,' the man replied. 'And anyway, the stun gun would punch straight through.'

Jarli was back on the phone. 'Mr Plowman—

you said there would be a manual off-switch on the robot,' he said. 'There must be a way to get to that switch without the robot shooting us on sight. Right? Otherwise, what's the point of having a switch in the first place?'

'I assume the robot has facial recognition software.' Plowman opened a plastic crate and started rummaging through the pieces inside. 'It will be programmed to recognise Viper, and anyone else he trusts to manage the robot. So Viper and his people can get close enough to turn it off at the switch, but the robot will shoot anyone else who tries.'

'So we need to add our faces to the database somehow.'

'Again, we'd need to hack an unhackable network for that.'

'Well, maybe we . . .' Jarli trailed off. Plowman could sense his desperation. 'Electromagnetic pulse. We use an EMP to shut down the robot.'

'I was thinking along exactly the same lines,' Plowman said, still digging through the box.

'The robot will just restart itself,' the man put in.

'But that will take time,' the girl said. 'Correct?'

'Fifteen minutes, give or take.'

'OK,' Jarli said. 'We hit the building with an EMP. We go in, grab Doug and my Dad, and get out. We'll just need to generate the pulse somehow . . . Mr Plowman, do you have a microwave oven we can use? And some heavy metals?'

Plowman lifted a metal tube out of the box and blew the dust off, revealing the letters EPFC.

'No,' he said. 'But I have an explosive-pump flux compressor.'

A pause.

'That'll work,' Jarli said.

NOT ALONE

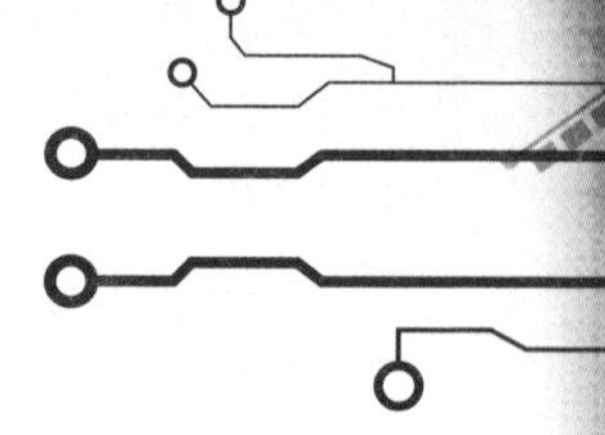

Detective Zee Arno crouched behind her car, watching as Dana Reynolds knocked on the double doors of the Kelton cinema. There were no lights on inside, and the street was deserted.

The tap on the journalist's phone had been a wash. Her calls were encrypted. But the location tracking had worked, and Arno had been able to follow Reynolds here.

Reynolds didn't wait for anyone to answer the door. She pushed it open and disappeared into the cinema.

Arno hesitated. If she followed, she could be walking into a TRAP. But if she didn't, she was unlikely to learn anything. And Viper's deadline was less than eight hours away.

She stood up and ran towards the doors.

The inside of the cinema was dark except for a trickle of light from the streetlamp outside. The carpet was sticky. Arno crept past the box office, an abandoned popcorn machine and a row of posters before entering the first of the two theatres.

It was deathly silent, rows of seats and dusty velvet curtains absorbing all the sound. The blank screen loomed over the room, monolithic. No sign of Reynolds.

Arno edged back out, and then snuck over to the other theatre. She could hear voices from inside.

'Anything?'

'No. I thought this might be a good spot.'

'Why?'

'The video was . . . theatrical.'

Arno needed to know who was in there. She eased around the corner. The other theatre was larger than the first. Reynolds was standing in the aisle. Someone else was bent over, looking under the seats. When she stood up, Arno recognised her: former Constable Irena Blanco.

Arno leaned back, staying in the shadows. Blanco was a severe-looking woman with dark, watchful eyes and a chipped tooth. She had been suspended when her partner was caught working for Viper. Most people in the department assumed she had been involved too. No-one had managed to prove it so far. But whenever Viper was up to something, Blanco had a way of showing up.

If Blanco was Reynolds's source, that explained how Reynolds had found out where Arno lived.

Blanco had given her a ride home from work once.

'If not here, where?' Reynolds asked.

'Somewhere high,' Blanco said. 'For good dispersal. There's no way of knowing exactly where in Kelton the target will be.'

'The roof?'

Her heart pounding, Detective Arno reached into her pocket and pulled out a phone.

'I talked to your former colleague,' Reynolds was saying. 'Arno. She doesn't seem to know anything.'

'That doesn't surprise me much—hey, did you hear that?'

The sound had been the click of Arno unlocking her phone. Holding her breath, she edged backwards out of the theatre.

She heard Blanco whisper, 'We're not alone in here.'

'You go that way, I'll go this way.'

Arno reached the foyer and broke into a run. She had almost reached the front doors, when—

'Freeze.'

Arno stopped and put her hands up.

'Turn around.'

Arno did. She found the former constable pointing a stun gun at her.

'Detective.' Blanco looked surprised. She quickly holstered her weapon. 'What are you doing here?'

'What are *you* doing here?' Arno countered.

'You're a civilian. You should be long gone.'

'I'm suspended. Not a civilian.'

Reynolds appeared behind Blanco. She watched this exchange, saying nothing.

'Either way,' Arno said, 'you should have left town.'

'You think I work for Viper,' Blanco said. 'So does everyone else.'

'The fact that you're still here, looking for somewhere to plant the botulism—'

'This is Viper's endgame. Destroy Kelton. Once that's done, he'll disappear.'

Arno glanced at Reynolds.

'Catching Viper is the only way to clear my name,' Blanco continued. 'And this is my last chance.'

'You expect me to believe that you're here to prove your innocence?'

'I don't expect you to believe it,' Blanco said. 'But it's the truth.'

Arno couldn't see her face in the dim light. But she sounded choked up. An innocent woman—or an excellent actress.

'I have to get back to work,' Arno said. She turned towards the double doors.

Viper would shoot me in the back, she thought. She took one step towards the door.

Two steps.

Three.

CRASH-LANDING

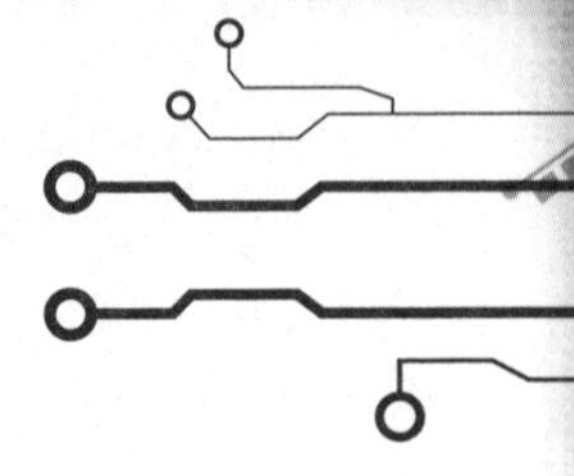

At 5 a.m., rain started to fall.

The streets were deserted. Those who could leave Kelton had left. Those who couldn't, or had decided not to, were inside with the doors and windows locked. This had always been a quiet town, but Jarli had never known it to be silent.

This is what it will be like after the botulism is released, he thought. *Unless we stop it.*

The windows were smashed at the chemist and the supermarket. People had been stocking up on antibiotics, food and water, Jarli guessed. The broken glass gave the street an apocalyptic vibe.

'Tread carefully,' Plowman said. He was shivering, despite the blanket he'd been wrapped in when they met up with him.

Anya and Jarli used their phones as torches, treading between the glittering shards. Scanner's phone dinged, and he checked the screen. 'We have a problem.'

'Yay,' Jarli muttered.

'My handler is telling me to evacuate. All the other troops are being pulled out as well.'

'What?' Anya said. 'Why?'

'The new Assistant Minister for Defence is a friend. Apparently her boss has given the order to drop a thermobaric warhead on Kelton. He—'

A fist of fear clenched Jarli's heart. 'A *what?*'

'It will carbonise the botulism, making it harmless.'

'But what about the people?'

'Also carbonised, along with the buildings, and a lot of the surrounding bushland. Hence the evac. Come on.'

Scanner turned to go back the way they had come.

'They can't drop a bomb on their own country,' Plowman said.

'They can and they do. They tested one of those warheads only a hundred kilometres from here last year.'

'Dad.' Anya grabbed Scanner's arm. 'Wait.'

Scanner shook her off. 'Orders are orders.'

'There are still people in town,' Jarli said. 'Like my dad, and Doug, and probably a lot of others. People who didn't hear the warnings. We have to help them.'

'That's not our job.'

'That's *exactly* your job. Protecting people.'

Scanner ignored this. He was looking over Jarli's shoulder. 'Anya,' he yelled. 'Wait!'

Anya was walking up the street, deeper into the town centre. Towards the prison.

Scanner chased after her. 'Stop right there.'

Anya didn't. 'I am going to save those prisoners. You can leave without me.'

Scanner ground his teeth. 'You know I won't do that.'

'Then it is settled.' She looked him up and down. 'Unless you are going to try to drag me back to the car?'

For a moment, Scanner looked like he was prepared to do exactly that.

'What time is the warhead supposed to drop?' Jarli asked quickly.

'11 a.m.,' Scanner said evenly.

'It'll take fifteen minutes to search the prison. Twenty at the most. That's all the time we need.'

'It's all the time we have,' Plowman pointed out. 'If we can't find the robot, it will wake up fifteen minutes after the EMP.'

Scanner ground his teeth.

'And if we find the botulism,' Jarli said, 'they'll call off the warhead. The town is saved, along with everyone in it.'

Scanner jabbed a finger at Jarli, then Plowman, and finally Anya. 'Fifteen minutes,' he said. 'And not one second more. You got that?'

Everyone nodded. But Jarli worried that it wouldn't be enough time, despite what he'd said. Throwaway was a big building. What if the botulism was there, and they didn't find it?

They ran past the town hall and slowed down as they approached the library. Scanner held up a fist, and Anya stopped immediately. Jarli bumped into the back of her, and Plowman bumped into him.

'What's happening?' Jarli whispered. In the deathly silence of the street, even a WHISPER felt loud.

'Throwaway is just around this corner,' Scanner said. 'Are we close enough to set up the EMP?'

'I think so.' Plowman took the tube out of his bag and screwed it onto a folding tripod, talking as he worked. 'There will be an explosion at this end which compresses the helix coil in the centre, and trips the load-switch here. That will send a blast of electromagnetic energy towards—'

'Do we need to know this?' Scanner asked.

'I'm just saying, it can only be used once,' Plowman replied. 'I don't have the time or the materials to make a second compressor. We only get one shot.'

'Copy that.' Scanner turned to Jarli. 'Once we get the door open, you and Plowman will have to turn right, go up two flights of stairs, then take a left at the end of the corridor. That's where I saw your father.'

'What about you and Anya?' Jarli said. 'Shouldn't we stick together?'

Scanner shook his head. 'We'll be heading for the charging station. If we can get to the robot before it reboots, then we can hit the off-switch. Make sure it doesn't get us on our way out.'

Anya looked concerned about this plan. 'Mr Plowman is the robot expert,' she said. 'Maybe we should swap.'

'True, but I'm the searching buildings expert,' Scanner said. 'Glen Durras will only trust Jarli—and I want an adult in each group. Don't question my orders.'

Anya bit her lip and nodded.

'What if Viper left some human guards behind?' Plowman asked.

'He didn't,' Scanner said. 'That was the point of the robot—so he could get his people out of town before the botulism is released, without leaving the prisoners unguarded.'

Jarli nodded slowly. 'OK. Let's go rescue my dad.'

Plowman had finished setting up the device on

the tripod, but he couldn't move it with his arm in a sling. Jarli and Anya carried the tripod around the corner.

As the building came into sight—a menacing concrete slab—Jarli started to feel queasy. He couldn't get rid of the sense that if he went inside, he would never find his way out again.

But Dad was in there. So Jarli took a deep breath and angled the tube towards the building.

He cleared his throat. 'You really think this will work?'

'The EMP?' Plowman asked. 'Sure. But after that, I have no idea. Anything could happen.'

He looked oddly excited by this prospect.

'Great,' Jarli said, gloomily.

Plowman's finger hovered over the switch. He glanced at the others. 'You, uh, might want to stand back.'

Everyone backed away.

'Actually,' Plowman said, 'I forgot about my pacemaker. *I'd* better stand back.'

'You forgot you had a pacemaker?' Scanner said incredulously.

Plowman ignored this. 'Jarli, you'll have to hit the switch.'

Nervously, Jarli swapped places with Plowman.

'Give me your phone,' Plowman said. 'So the

EMP doesn't fry it.'

Jarli tossed his phone over. As always, he felt instantly vulnerable without it—but also lighter. More free.

He put his finger on the orange switch that Plowman had been about to push. 'This one?'

'Yes.' Plowman had his fingers in his ears.

Jarli took a deep breath, and pushed the button.

There was a sharp *crack,* like a gunshot. The compressor jolted, and the tripod fell over. A hole had burned through the tube, leaking smoke. Jarli felt his hair standing on end.

He coughed and waved away the smoke. 'Did it work?'

'There's no way to be sure,' Plowman said. 'We'll just have to hope for—'

Smash! An object the size of a motorbike crash-landed in the middle of the street. Shards of metal and plastic went flying. When the debris settled, Jarli realised it was one of Plowman's drones. It had fallen out of the sky, and now lay on the road like a dead pterodactyl.

'Well, it worked on that,' Anya observed.

'Fifteen minutes starts now,' Scanner said. 'Go!'

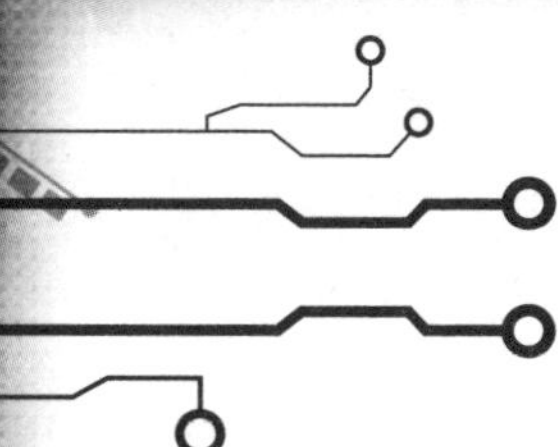

FIFTEEN CENTIMETRES OF STEEL

'Wait,' Jarli puffed, as they sprinted towards the prison. 'We have to enter through that alley. There's a secret tunnel through the wall. This place doesn't have a door.'

'It does now,' Scanner said. 'Viper installed one when he took over. And he sealed the tunnel.'

He was right. As they got closer, Jarli saw a steel door inset in the concrete. There was a keypad mounted on the wall next to it.

'Won't it be locked?'

'There's a six digit code and a thumbprint scanner. I'm authorised, so it will let me in.'

'No it won't. We just fried the electronics with an EMP.'

Scanner looked back at Plowman, who nodded.

'It'll let you in when the system reboots,' Plowman said. 'But by then the robot will be awake.'

'We could have thought this through a bit better,' Anya observed.

'We'll have to break down the door.' Jarli lifted

his foot to kick it.

'The steel is fifteen centimetres thick,' Scanner said. 'There's no way you—'

Bang! Jarli's foot hit the handle, and the door swung inwards. It hit the wall inside with a clang that echoed through the dark interior of the prison.

'Huh,' Scanner said. 'Viper left it unlocked.'

'Or,' Anya said, 'we're not the first people to break in today.'

They all looked uneasily at one another.

'The plan stays the same,' Scanner said finally. 'Jarli, Plowman, you get the prisoners. Anya, you're with me. We need to get to that robot within the next—' He checked his watch. '—fourteen minutes, six seconds, and stop it from waking up.'

Jarli took his phone back from Plowman and switched on the torch app. He shone it into the prison, illuminating the thick concrete walls.

The prisoners had named this place Throwaway, as in, 'throw away the key'. But the name could also describe the INMATES. While he had been imprisoned here, Jarli had felt like he was the one who had been thrown away. Like he was buried alive in a landfill somewhere.

Anya touched his arm, and he flinched.

'Are you OK?' she asked.

Jarli nodded. Dad and Doug were counting on

him. 'Fine. Let's do this.'

He crept into the darkness and turned right, towards the stairs. Plowman followed. Anya and Scanner went the other way.

Thirteen minutes, fourteen seconds. Jarli hoped it would be enough.

PART TWO: UNMASKED

THE APP DOESN'T ACTUALLY DETECT LIES—IT DETECTS THE INTENT TO DECEIVE. SO EVEN IF SOMEONE SAYS SOMETHING THAT'S TECHNICALLY TRUE, THE APP MAY STILL CALL IT A LIE IF THE PERSON SOUNDS LIKE THEY'RE NERVOUS, OR PAUSES BEFORE ANSWERING. BUT THAT ALSO MEANS THAT A BRILLIANT PSYCHOPATH—SOMEONE WHO DOESN'T GET NERVOUS AND DOESN'T HAVE TO PAUSE TO THINK—COULD FOOL IT. I'M WORKING ON THE PROBLEM.

—From the documentation for Truth, *version 5.2*

IT MIGHT HAVE BEEN REVENGE

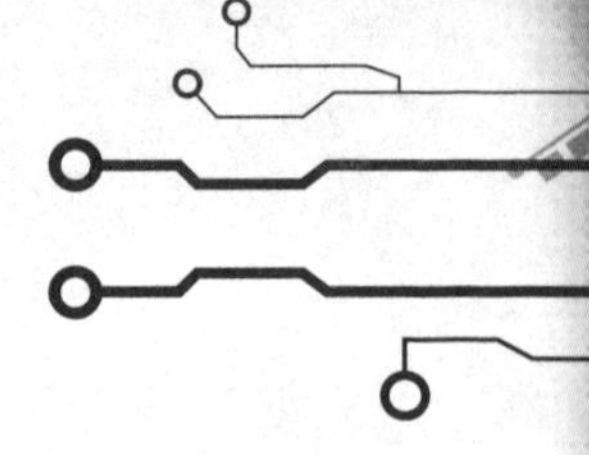

Jarli crept up the stairs, Plowman following behind. They had to hurry, but they also wanted to stay quiet. Jarli didn't believe Viper would have left the door unlocked, so someone must have broken in—and they might still be here. Maybe they were just looking for supplies of water, food or medicine . . . but maybe not.

Jarli's phone rang. He jumped, and fumbled for a moment before answering.

It was Bess. 'Not a great time,' he said.

'Please tell me you made it out of Kelton,' she said.

'Um, not exactly.'

'Jarli!'

'My dad is still here,' he said. 'And Doug. I have to find them.'

'Tell the police to find them. That's their job.'

'The police have been told to leave town because a bomb is about to be dropped on it. And you know Viper has people in the police force.'

'Did you say bomb?!'

'Yeah. It'll destroy the botulism, but also pretty much everything else. Including Doug and Dad.'

Silence trickled down the line.

'What can I do?' Bess asked finally.

'Are you in Axe Falls? Safe?'

'Yeah.'

'We think the botulism canister might be in Throwaway—the old prison. But if we're wrong, we need more places to search. If we can work out who Viper is, we might be able to retrace his steps using Plowman's drone network.'

'We've been trying to identify him for a year now.'

'I know,' Jarli said. 'But now we have some extra clues. I've been thinking about the burns on his face. Maybe you could try to find a list of Kelton locals—or at least, people from this country—who were injured like that in recent wars.'

'Why wars? Why not a kitchen fire, or an industrial accident?'

'Because Viper tried to kill Fisher, the Minister for Defence. Remember?'

'You think it might have been revenge,' Bess said slowly. 'Fisher sends our troops into a war zone, Viper gets half his face burned off, then he comes home and blames Fisher.'

'Something like that,' Jarli said.

'How does that fit with the other parts of his operation? Like giving new identities to criminals?'

'Viper couldn't murder a government minister by himself and get away with it. He would need people, and money. Every time he gives someone a new face and a new identity, they pay him—and he puts a chip in them so they have to do whatever he says.'

'What about stealing the RCG?' Bess asked. 'The thing he used to crash a plane into Doug's house?'

'Kelton is on a major flight path. Maybe he wanted to shoot down Fisher's plane next time he flew over the town.'

'So why is he trying to destroy Kelton?'

'I don't know,' Jarli said. 'I just know we have to stop him.'

'OK,' Bess said. 'I'll do some research, and let you know what I dig up.'

'Good luck.'

'You too. Please make sure you're out of Kelton by noon, OK?'

'OK,' Jarli said, and ended the call.

'Was that Bess?' Plowman asked.

'Yeah. How do you know about Bess?'

'You've mentioned her before.'

Jarli didn't remember that. 'Oh. Well, she's going to do some digging. See if she can figure out who

Viper is, so we know where else to search for the botulism.'

'The police task force has never even come close. Do you really think a teenage girl will succeed?'

'If anyone can, it's her.' They had reached the cell block. He looked around, the MEMORIES attacking him from all sides. His imprisonment had lasted less than twenty-four hours, but it had felt like months. The helplessness had been crushing. No phone. No friends. No way out.

He walked around, shining his torch into each of the cells.

'Dad?' he called. 'It's me, Jarli!'

No answer.

'Doug?'

Nothing.

Jarli reached the last cell. It was empty.

His father and Doug were missing.

A GLOWING RED LIGHT

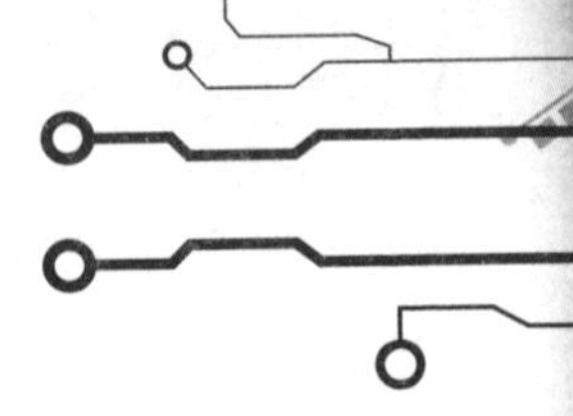

'This is bad.'

Anya looked around. 'What?'

Her father shone his torch on a flat black disc, about the size of a set of bathroom scales. A small red light glowed on one side. 'This is the wireless charging station,' he said. 'When the robot isn't active, it should be here.'

'It must have been walking around when the EMP deactivated it,' Anya said. 'Right?'

'Right. So that means something else triggered it before we arrived.'

Anya peered into the shadows. 'We are not alone in here then.'

'Right. And the robot could be anywhere. We have less than . . . nine minutes before it wakes up.'

Anya couldn't see her father's face in the dark. 'We'll have to split up,' she said.

'I agree.'

There was a pause.

'Be careful, Anya,' he said, and then started

walking away towards a row of offices.

He would never say *I love you*. The closest he ever got was *be careful*.

Anya turned the other way. Her father had said a break room was nearby. She wove through some junk—a dusty mop and bucket, an abandoned computer chair, and a window with brackets for a curtain rail, but no curtain. She was two floors above the ground—from up here she should have been able to see the lights all over Kelton. But there was only darkness behind the glass.

She had to make allowances for her father. His mission required 100 per cent of his attention, day and night. She'd once overheard him talking to her mother, through the thin walls of their townhouse: 'Emotion is distraction. And distraction is the first step towards a mistake. One that could cost you, or me, or Anya our lives.'

Anya had accompanied him on missions before, but this—searching a building for a deadly robot hours before the release of a lethal neurotoxin—had higher stakes than usual. She would have thought some show of humanity was appropriate.

If Anya had been in his position, she would have taken the opportunity to tell her daughter she was proud. She knew he had said it to her sister, before she died. Maybe he believed the words were cursed.

Even in the dark, the small break room didn't take long to search. She checked under the table, behind the waste bin, in the dead-end tunnel hidden behind the fridge. No sign of the robot. And she only had six minutes before it woke up.

There was a bathroom right next door. She searched it. All the cubicles were empty. There was a shower, too. Also empty.

Something clattered elsewhere in the building.

'Dad?' she called, poking her head back into the corridor. 'Is that you?'

The clattering stopped. No-one responded. Then there was a hissing, whirring sound. Something mechanical.

Suddenly Anya realised something she should have figured out much earlier. *Distraction is the first step towards a mistake.*

If the EMP had knocked out all the electronics, then why had there been **A GLOWING RED LIGHT** on the charging station?

Hiss. Thump. Hiss. Thump.

The obvious explanation was that the station had some kind of shielding which protected it from the EMP.

And if that was possible, the robot would have shielding, too.

Hiss. Thump.

A shadow appeared at the far end of the corridor. Not a human shape. Something out of a nightmare. Like a mechanical wolf.

Anya ducked back into the bathroom, heart pounding. The robot was already patrolling again. She could hear it getting closer and closer to the bathroom.

She scurried into one of the cubicles and softly closed the door. She sat on the lid of the toilet and braced her feet against the inside of the door to keep them out of sight.

Hiss. Thump. The robot was inside the room.

RECORD MISSING

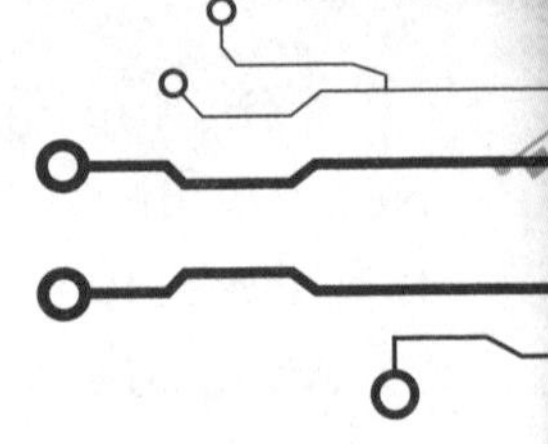

'Closed!' the librarian said, pointing at the sign with a pudgy finger. His voice was muffled by the glass.

Bess kept knocking. 'Please!' She shivered as though it were cold outside, and made sure her crutches were in full view. Sometimes people let her bend the rules, feeling sorry for her.

Not this guy. 'We don't open for another two hours,' he said. '*I* shouldn't even be here.'

He had opened a dialogue. *First mistake,* Bess thought.

'But since you *are* here,' she said, 'you can let me in! I'll be quiet. You won't even know I'm there.'

This would have worked on the librarian in Kelton, a friendly lady named Jasmine who was used to Bess hanging around at odd hours. But in Axe Falls, apparently the library staff were made of sterner stuff.

'Young lady, I appreciate your enthusiasm for the library. I do. But it will still be here at 8 a.m.'

Bess gritted her teeth. After evacuating Kelton

and unpacking their things at the hotel, it had been almost impossible to convince her mother to drop her off at the library. It would all be for nothing if she couldn't get through this door. 'Please. I really, really, *really* need to look some stuff up. Urgently.'

She thought she could see a glimmer of sympathy in his expression. Something to build on.

'There are some things you just can't find on the internet,' she added.

Although he tried to hide it, the librarian seemed to warm to this.

'All right,' he said gruffly, hitting the green button next to the door. 'But no borrowing until I've got the computers up and running. Understood?'

Bess nodded eagerly as the doors slid aside. 'Thank you so much!'

The librarian shook his head and walked back over to his work station. He moved his cup of tea and his biscuit out of sight, but not before Bess saw them.

Bess hobbled past the children's section, where a huge model pirate ship was perched atop the bookshelves. After the large-print section she spotted a sign that said 'archived news'. Not her usual area—she would normally be reading classic novels or new fantasy releases. But Jarli had given her an important mission: find a list of people who were burned in recent wars. And what she had told the librarian was true. There was so much information in cyberspace that it was easy not to notice what *wasn't* there.

Her web searching had given her a starting point, though. There was a publication for veterans which included lists of people who'd received medals after injuries in battle. Hopefully the lists had been digitised, so she could search them quickly.

At first, she thought she was in luck. The library did have digitised copies of the publication. Bess logged into one of the computers using her Kelton library account, and started bringing up pages from various editions.

Then her luck ran out. There were lists of wounded soldiers, but it didn't say what the injuries were, or which state the soldiers came from. And even if Bess read all the lists, hoping to recognise the name of someone in Kelton, there was no guarantee that Viper would be listed. He could have been a civilian, or perhaps a soldier from another country. It was hopeless.

But since she was here . . .

Bess typed the word VIPER into a search field. Just in case.

And something came up.

Record missing.

Bess twisted the screen towards the librarian's desk. 'Excuse me.'

The librarian looked up. 'You said you'd be quiet.'

'What does this mean?' Bess asked.

The librarian shuffled over, frowning. 'Huh. That's not right.'

'What's happened?'

'It looks like that issue has been erased from the digital catalogue. But that's not supposed to be possible.'

A tingle ran up Bess's spine. Viper had a habit of making impossible things happen. 'Do you still have the paper version?' she asked.

The librarian glanced at a door marked *Archive*. 'Customers aren't supposed to—'

'I can help you find the issue so you can re-upload it,' Bess said. 'You'd have to do that anyway, right? It'll be quicker with my help.'

The librarian sighed and pulled some keys out of his pocket. 'Follow me.'

NOT EVEN YOURSELF

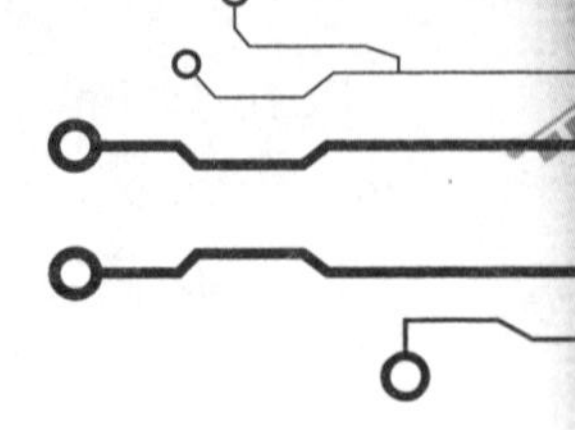

'I don't understand.' Jarli shone his torch around the cell block. 'Where could they have gone?'

'Are there any other cells in the building?' Plowman asked.

'Yes, but Scanner said they were empty. All those prisoners were loaded onto a transport truck.' Jarli checked his watch. Two minutes until the robot was due to wake up. He hoped Anya and Scanner had found it.

Plowman raised a finger. 'Possibility number one: they escaped.' He held up two fingers. 'Possibility two: Viper moved them somewhere else. Possibility three.' He raised a third finger. 'They were never here in the first place.'

Jarli's heart sank. 'You're saying Scanner can't be trusted.'

'Think about it. What do you really know about him?'

'Not much. But my phone has been on the whole time. He can't lie.'

'You already know Viper and his people can beat the app,' Plowman said.

'*Truth Premium,* sure—but not my original version.'

Something shifted in the darkness behind Plowman. A human figure grew out of the shadows.

Jarli stepped backwards. 'Watch out!' he cried.

Plowman whirled around. 'Who goes there?'

'Take it easy. It's me.' Maria Eaton, the school nurse, emerged from the shadows.

Jarli sagged with relief. 'What are you doing here? I thought you were leaving town.'

'I am,' Eaton said. 'But two people were being held prisoner here. I came to get them out.'

'How did you know about this place?'

'I'm the one who told your friends about it, remember?'

This was true. Jarli had been able to expose Throwaway in part because Eaton had told Doug and Bess about it.

Eaton looked over her shoulder. 'We have to be careful. There's an attack-robot on the loose.'

'We shut it down with an EMP,' Plowman said.

'No, you didn't. It's still walking around. It must have been shielded somehow. But you killed all the security cameras, so it's taking a long time to find you.'

'Are they OK?' Jarli said. 'My dad and Doug?'

Eaton nodded. 'I got them out of their cells. They're on their way out of town. But there's something I have to tell you.' She glanced from Jarli to Plowman, looking troubled.

'Can it wait until we get out of here?' Jarli asked.

'Not really.' Eaton turned to Plowman. 'I've been thinking about your scar. Viper didn't perform the surgery in person, right?'

'No,' Plowman said. 'He used a remote-control robot.'

'Are you *certain* that it was remote controlled, rather than autonomous? A robot programmed to do brain surgery by itself?'

'I suppose that's possible,' Plowman said slowly. 'But Viper would need to know a lot about robots to pull that off.'

'I agree.' Eaton looked him up and down. 'Imagine you're Viper—the head of a huge criminal network. Imagine someone made a lie-detector app which threatened to expose you. What could you do to hide from it?'

'Well, I could do what Viper did—release my own version of the app,' Plowman said. 'And program it to recognise my voice and tell users that everything I said was true.'

'That wouldn't protect you from anyone using the original version. Or any future versions.

But there would be one way to make sure no-one would ever find out the truth. Not even yourself.'

'I don't understand.'

'Take a look at this.' Eaton walked into one of the cells and crouched down next to the wall. Jarli and Plowman followed her in.

'See that?' She pointed into the corner.

Plowman frowned. 'No.'

Eaton stepped back, moving out of the way so Plowman could get a closer look. Then she grabbed Jarli and dragged him back out of the cell. She SLAMMED the door. The lock clicked.

Plowman spun around. 'Hey! What are you doing?!'

'The best way to protect yourself,' Eaton said, 'would be to erase your own memory. You wouldn't need to lie, because you wouldn't even know you were guilty.'

CAGED ANIMAL

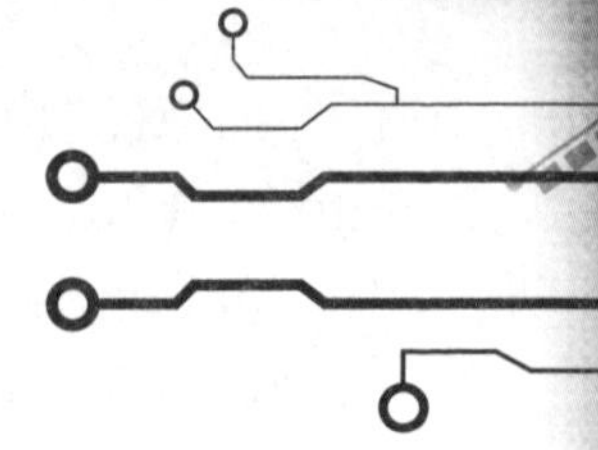

'Let me out this instant!' Plowman demanded. He grabbed the bars of the cell and shook them, but they didn't even rattle.

Jarli stared at Eaton, mouth agape.

'Think about it, Jarli,' she said. 'Viper is brilliant. Rich. Good with computers and robots. Anti-government. Seems to know everything. Does that sound familiar?'

'But Plowman has been helping me track down Viper,' Jarli said.

'Since the surgery erased his memories. Right?'

'I . . .' Jarli's heartbeat was getting louder in his ears.

'If Plowman knew who he was hunting,' Eaton said, 'he might not have been so helpful.'

'This is ridiculous!' Plowman bellowed. 'I am not Viper!'

Jarli looked down at his phone. He'd come to depend on the app. 'It says he's telling the truth.'

'He thinks he *is* telling the truth,' Eaton said. 'But

ask yourself if an innocent man would have drones surveilling the whole town. Ask yourself why Viper didn't just kill Plowman, or make him disappear. That's what Viper did to the other people who got in his way.'

'But what about the video, where he threatened the town?'

'The burned face was a mask. And there's no proof that the video wasn't recorded weeks ago.'

'I'm warning you,' Plowman snarled.

Eaton turned to face him. 'Warning me of what? What will you do if I don't let you out? Your memories may be gone, but your personality hasn't changed. Are you feeling the urge to hurt me? Kill me?'

'Jarli.' Plowman's face had darkened with rage. 'This is madness. Let me out of here.'

Jarli agreed. This *was* madness. And yet, everything Eaton had said made sense.

Something else occurred to him. He had assumed the botulism canister would be placed somewhere high, so that it could explode and shower the surrounding buildings with the deadly toxin. But if Plowman was Viper, he would use a drone. Something which could fly over the whole town, raining death.

'We can't just leave him here,' Jarli said weakly.

'The prison is airtight,' Eaton said. 'If we close

the door, the toxin won't get to him.'

'Don't listen to her, Jarli,' Plowman insisted. 'She's lying.'

Not according to Jarli's phone. 'My app says—'

'Then someone else has deceived her. Get me out of here!'

Eaton pointed at a green button on the wall. 'It's your call, Jarli,' she said. 'You know him better than I do. If you really think he's innocent, let him out. But I don't know what he'll do.'

Jarli hesitated, looking at the button. If he let Plowman out, he could be freeing Viper. But if he didn't, he could be leaving an INNOCENT man in prison. And no-one in this room knew the truth, not even Plowman himself.

'We'll come back for you,' he said finally.

'No!' Plowman screamed, and kicked the bars.

'You'll be safe here while we search for the botulism. We—'

'Don't do this! Jarli!'

Jarli swallowed, and turned away.

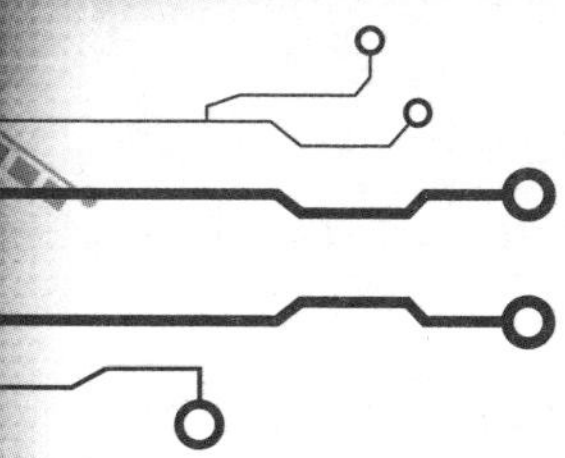

POTENTIALLY USEFUL PRISONER

'Look.'

Glen was pointing at the old petrol station. The sign above it was dark, and the lights were off inside. But Doug could see that one of the windows was broken.

'What?' he asked.

'They would sell phones,' Glen said. 'Cheap ones.'

When the school nurse had found them and let them out of their cells, neither of them had asked if they could borrow her phone. They had been too surprised. Too grateful.

Until she told them that the whole town was about to be drenched in deadly particles. Then they had been too scared.

Doug wished Eaton had come with them. But she had said she wanted to search the rest of the building. He had been relieved when she didn't ask them to stay and help.

For Doug, the truth didn't sink in until he saw the empty streets and the looted shops. They had been walking for kilometres, and hadn't seen a soul. Occasionally they heard footsteps or voices, but the sounds always turned out to be their own echoes.

Even if the botulism wasn't released, Viper had already won. He had killed this town.

'We need to keep moving,' Doug said.

Glen checked his plastic wristwatch. 'We still have a couple of hours before the toxin is dispersed.'

'You trust Viper not to release it early?'

Glen hesitated. Apparently this hadn't occurred to him. 'Why would he do that?'

'By accident. Or if he thinks the police are getting close. Or just because he's evil.'

Glen started to move towards the petrol station. 'We'll be quick. We need to call our families.'

Doug grabbed his arm. 'We don't have time.' He was desperate to hear his mother's voice. But he knew she would want him to get to safety as fast as possible.

'If we don't call them, they might come back into town looking for us,' Glen insisted. 'Then they could get trapped here when the toxin is released.'

Doug put his face in his hands. Glen was right. Also, Doug hadn't told him that he had been replaced—that there was a fake Glen Durras with his family right now. Doug hadn't wanted to upset him. But it was important that they warn Jarli if they could.

'OK, OK,' Doug said. 'But we have to be *really* quick.'

Glen hadn't waited for Doug's permission. He was already running towards the petrol station.

Doug followed Glen past the air hoses and petrol pumps and across a puddle of petrol—someone had left a nozzle dangling. Doug tried the door. Locked.

'Watch your head.' Glen clambered through the broken window.

Doug followed, hunched over to keep clear of the spikes of glass that hung from the top of the frame like stalactites.

The inside of the petrol station looked like a garbage dump. There was more stuff on the floor than on the shelves. All the water and most of the food had been taken. Someone had cut through the wires over the counter and taken all the cash out of the till. Doug found that strangely unsettling. Money wasn't essential for survival, like food or water, but the thieves had taken it anyway. Just because they could.

'I don't know how we're going to find a phone in all this,' he said.

Glen was already on his hands and knees, pushing aside magazines and CDs. 'We just have to try.'

They both rummaged through the junk. Cheap toys. Boxes of tissues. Matches. Batteries. When

Doug found a packet of chips—cheese and onion flavour—it was hard not to rip it open. He hadn't eaten anything other than brown rice since he'd been imprisoned. He resolved to take it with him when he left—then he wondered if that made him as bad as the people who had emptied the till. After all, he wasn't starving. He didn't need the chips to live.

There was no sign of a phone. Burner phones were useful enough that they had probably all been taken already.

'I don't think—' Doug began.

And then headlights swept across the window.

Doug instinctively flattened himself against the floor.

'What—' Glen began.

'Down!'

As Glen crouched down, a black 4WD parked between the shop and one of the petrol bowsers. A tall man in a flannel shirt got out of the ute and grabbed one of the pumps. As he turned to put the nozzle into the tank, Doug saw his face.

It was Glen Durras. No, Doug quickly realised—it was the man Viper had replaced him with.

The real Glen saw the face too, and let out a gasp. 'Who is that?!'

'Shh!' Doug hissed back.

The man's head snapped around to face the

shop. He stood still for a long moment. Then he started walking towards the shop, leaving the nozzle plugged into his ute.

Doug looked around frantically for a place to hide. Behind the counter was too obvious, and they would have to walk past the window to get there. A nearby door was marked **STAFF ONLY,** but Doug could see muddy footprints next to the handle. Someone had tried and failed to kick it open.

'Bury yourself!' Doug hissed. He started digging deeper into the junk all over the floor, like a fox trying to tunnel under a fence. When he reached the floor he lay on his back and dragged debris onto his body. Hopefully Glen was doing the same thing.

They were out of time. Doug lay still as he heard the man crunch into the room.

Cobra peered around the dark interior of the petrol station. He was sure he'd heard something. It could have been an animal, rummaging around in all the rubbish on the floor, looking for food. But it could also have been a person.

'Hello?' he called out. 'Can anybody help me? I'm having trouble with my car.'

Silence. Either no-one was in here, or someone

was in here, but they knew who he was, so they weren't coming out.

The Durras kid and his friends. It had to be.

Cobra climbed in the window and trudged through the debris into the first aisle, looking for hiding places. He had intended to be long gone by now. Soon Viper would realise that Cobra's cover was blown and that he had lost the kid. Viper would remotely trigger the POISON capsule in Cobra's hand. Cobra's plan had been to dump his phone, collect his secret getaway vehicle—the one Viper didn't know about—and drive deep into the desert, where there was no coverage. Hopefully he would be out of range before Viper sent the signal. Then Cobra could find a doctor or a vet who might remove the capsule without asking too many questions. The two million dollars in cash he'd saved up over the years would probably help.

But if the kid and his friends were still in Kelton, he could capture them and lock them in the spacious boot of his 4WD. Then he could call Viper and ask what to do with them. Viper might be annoyed that Cobra's false identity had been exposed, but he wouldn't poison Cobra over it. Not when Cobra had a potentially useful prisoner or two.

No-one was hiding in the first aisle of the shop. Cobra turned the corner, passing the giant coffee machine, and entered the second aisle.

He was unarmed, but Jarli was small. And if there were others, Cobra could pick Jarli up and use him like a human shield.

Something rustled in the debris at his feet. Cobra glanced down sharply. Had that been a rat, looking for scraps? Or was there a human shape under all those magazines and chip packets?

Cobra bent over—

And saw movement out of the corner of his eye.

He whirled around. But it was just a mirror in the corner. His own reflection, staring back.

Then his reflection charged.

Cobra nearly jumped out of his skin. He swore and stumbled backwards as his doppelganger—the real Glen Durras, he realised—sprinted through the shop towards him, an empty petrol can raised above his head. Durras's eyes were wild. Cobra couldn't tell if he was angry or terrified, or both.

Cobra tried to back away, but a hand snaked out of the rubbish at his feet and grabbed his ankle. He tripped and crashed into the shelves, knocking them down and landing on top of them.

He rolled over in time to see Glen Durras and a kid—one of Jarli's friends—pushing over the next row of shelves. They smashed down onto Cobra's legs, trapping him. Pain shot up his thighs. He struggled with the shelves, but couldn't get them off him.

'You're dead!' he screamed. 'You hear me? Dead!'

The two were already scrambling back out the broken window.

'Go!' Doug was yelling. 'Hurry!'

Glen was already sprinting towards the road. As Doug passed the black 4WD, he looked through the window and saw the keys in the ignition.

'Wait,' he said. 'We can take his car!'

'What about keys?'

'They're in here. Quick!'

Glen ran back and jumped in the driver's seat. Doug hopped in on the passenger side and looked in the rear view mirror. The fake Glen Durras hadn't come out of the building yet. He must still be trapped under the shelves.

The engine roared. With a screeching of tyres, the ute launched itself forward. The petrol nozzle ripped itself out of the tank with a squeal of metal on metal.

Doug watched as the station shrank in the mirror. Still no sign of the bad guy.

'That was a good plan,' he said. 'Distracting him

like that.'

'Plan?!' Glen was still trembling. 'I just saw a guy who had my face, and I grabbed the nearest solid object. Who *was* that?!'

In the mirror, Doug saw something on the back seat. He turned. His eyes widened.

'I don't know, exactly,' he said. 'But he was loaded.'

There was a clear plastic crate on the back seat. It was full of cash. Thousands of dollars, maybe millions. Doug was so entranced that it took him a minute to notice the item resting on top of the crate.

He reached over and picked it up. 'And hey,' he said. 'Now we have a phone.'

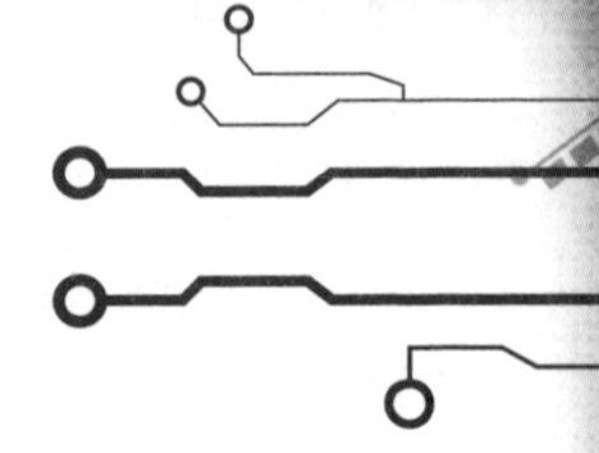

A FIZZING, BURNING SENSATION

Anya held her breath, her feet still braced against the cubicle door. There was no sound from the robot. Was it still in the bathroom? Or had it left so quietly she hadn't noticed?

That seemed impossible, given how much hissing and clanking it had made when it entered. But the robot wouldn't just be standing in the doorway, wondering what to do next. Robots didn't wonder. They made decisions in a microsecond. Actually, they didn't decide at all. They just did whatever they had been programmed to do.

So maybe this robot had been programmed to stand still and listen for a while. Anya tried to keep quiet, but her legs were cramping up. It was getting harder to resist the urge to move.

A minute turned into two, then three, then four.

Robots didn't get impatient, either. Anya was starting to worry that it was programmed to stand there until something else triggered it. Anya could be trapped in this bathroom for hours. She could still be here when the botulism was released.

Or worse, her father would come looking for her. He would call her name, and when she didn't answer, he would walk right into this bathroom. The robot would catch him by surprise.

It was this thought that got her moving. She had to do something.

She very carefully slipped a hand into her back pocket, where she always kept some coins.

The toilet seat creaked under her. She froze.

No sound from outside the cubicle. The robot hadn't heard, or didn't care, or wasn't there at all.

Only one way to be sure. She pulled out a ten-cent piece and chucked it over the right-hand wall into the next cubicle.

The coin chimed against the floor.

That got a reaction. With a sudden whirring and hissing, the robot stomped past Anya's cubicle, searching for the source of the sound. Anya watched under the cubicle door as the robot's carbon fibre claws scuttled past, left to right. Soon after it was out of sight, silence fell again. The robot had stopped moving.

It was closer now, so she had to be even quieter. But it wasn't between her and the exit anymore. There was a chance to escape. She couldn't open the cubicle door, though. It would see her.

Very carefully, Anya took her feet off the back of the door. She stood on the seat, braced one shoe against the toilet paper dispenser and grabbed the top of the left-hand cubicle wall.

It shouldn't have been a difficult climb. Anya was a skilled gymnast. But having to move silently made it almost impossible.

Almost. Wincing at every rustle of fabric and creak of chipboard, Anya hauled herself up onto the cubicle wall. She could see the exit. Freedom. Maybe she could even trap the robot in the bathroom, giving the others plenty of time to search the rest of the building.

Bang. She heard the robot smash open the door of the next cubicle along, where the coin was. Her cubicle might be next.

Anya dropped to the floor like a cat.

The robot heard. It immediately started towards her, joints clicking like maracas.

Anya sprinted for the exit. The robot *hiss-clanked* after her as she ran out the door and turned right, back towards where she had last seen her father. No time to try to shut the bathroom door—the robot was right behind her.

She pelted up the corridor, desperately looking for something she could use to defend herself. As she turned the corner, she saw a mop and bucket—

not much of a weapon. A window in the distance—not much of an escape route, given that she was two stories above the ground. A computer chair on wheels.

Individually, these things were useless. But together, they might just get her out of this.

The robot was gaining on her. She could hear a faint whine as its stun gun warmed up.

Anya snatched up the mop. The handle was plastic, not wood. Hopefully it would take her weight. As she ran, she kicked the computer chair as hard as she could. It rolled towards the window on squeaking wheels, but stopped halfway there.

Gritting her teeth, Anya caught up to the chair and kicked it again. This time it skidded all the way to the window and kept going, smashing the glass and plummeting out into the darkness.

Anya put on a burst of speed, sprinting towards the empty window frame. She held the mop horizontally above her head, like a chin-up bar.

Then she jumped, feet first.

She hurtled out the window, but the mop was longer than the window frame was wide. Both ends banged against the frame, jarring her shoulders in their sockets. The mop handle landed in the brackets, where the curtain rail should go. The brackets held Anya's weight.

She pulled her knees up to her chest just in time. The robot leapt at her and flew out the window, right under her heels. One of its outstretched claws brushed against her leg. There was a fizzing, burning sensation, and all Anya's limbs spasmed wildly. She lost her grip on the mop handle, and fell. Her torso thudded painfully onto the windowsill, and she gasped. She scrabbled at the frame and just managed to grab it in time.

The robot fell like a stone, and hit the concrete far below with a crash that echoed through the street. Looking down, Anya saw that parts of its carbon-fibre armour had SHATTERED, exposing the cables, hydraulics and steel skeleton underneath.

But it stood up, and started pacing back and forth next to the building. Looking for a way in. Anya was glad they had closed the door behind them. The robot seemed to be indestructible.

She hauled herself up over the windowsill and back into the corridor. She touched her chest gingerly. She would have some nasty bruises tomorrow, but she didn't think she had broken any ribs. She was lucky the chair and the robot had knocked out most of the glass—she could have ended up with a spike through the heart.

Be careful, Anya. Her father's voice echoed through her mind. She wondered if he would think she should have stayed in the bathroom.

Where *was* her father?

'Dad?' she called.

No answer.

Anya started hurrying back towards the offices her father had been searching. 'The robot is gone,' she called. 'But I did not find the canister anywhere. Where are you?'

She smelled anaesthetic from outside one of the offices and slowed. She pushed the door open and found her father face-down on the floor, splattered with anaesthetic, burn marks from a stun gun on his neck.

THE CELLS IN OUR LUNGS

'We have to get out of here,' Eaton said. 'Fast. Who else is in the building?'

She and Jarli had moved out of Plowman's earshot, but he wasn't out of theirs. They could hear him bellowing and kicking the bars in his cell.

Jarli still couldn't quite believe it. 'But if he's Viper—'

'There's no doubt in my mind,' Eaton said.

'Then shouldn't we be trying to make him tell us where the botulism canister is?'

'He doesn't know. He doesn't even think he is Viper. His surgery was very thorough. Even if we had something to bargain with, we wouldn't get any useful intel from him.'

Jarli touched the scab on the back of his own head. Now, more than ever, he wished he could remember what information had been removed from his brain.

'So what do we do, then?' he asked.

'Get out of Kelton. I can escort you most of

the way.'

'But what about the toxin?'

Eaton shrugged helplessly. 'Kelton is a small town, but not that small. I don't think you'll find it before it's released.'

'It's not going to be released,' Jarli said. 'The defence minister is planning to drop a bomb on the town.'

'He *what?*'

'He's trying to kill the botulism with a thermo-something or other warhead.'

The colour drained from Eaton's face. 'Thermonuclear?'

Jarli shook his head vigorously. 'No, something else.'

Eaton didn't look reassured. 'Thermobaric? A fuel-air bomb?'

'I think that was it. What does it do?'

'It's the most powerful non-nuclear explosive. If we're close to the detonation, we'll be vaporised. If we're further out, the shockwave will rupture the cells in our lungs, and we'll suffocate. When's the launch?'

'One hour before Viper's deadline,' Jarli said.

Eaton spat on the floor and wiped her mouth. 'That son of a . . . Fisher probably won't even evacuate the soldiers who are searching for the botulism.

He doesn't care if they live or die.'

'He did actually order the troops to leave.'

'Really? I wouldn't be so sure.'

Jarli had met Fisher before. He had seemed friendly and genuine. But later the façade had fallen away, revealing an angry, thoughtless man. Eaton was probably right.

'But he cares about his image,' Eaton continued, as if to herself. 'He's obsessed with it, in fact. If there's a public outcry, he won't drop the bomb. Can you get in touch with your journalist friend?'

'Reynolds? She's not really my—'

Anya appeared near the stairs. She was dragging her father along the ground.

'Help me!' she wheezed.

Jarli ran over. 'What happened?'

'The robot got him. Stunned him, and anaesthetised him.' Anya wiped the sweat out of her eyes. Jarli could tell how anxious she was. 'Do you think—' She noticed Eaton for the first time. 'Miss Eaton? What are you doing here?'

'I came here to tell Jarli that Kellin Plowman is Viper,' Eaton said bluntly. She crouched down next to Scanner's unconscious body. 'Did the robot get any anaesthetic on his face, or just here, on his hand?'

'I don't know, I didn't see . . . What do you mean,

Plowman is Viper?!'

Eaton just nodded.

'It's true,' Jarli said. 'We locked him in a cell back there. But he doesn't know where the botulism is—he erased his own memory.'

'He erased . . .' Anya shook her head, giving up.

'This is Anya's dad,' Jarli told Eaton. 'He's been investigating Viper with us. Can you help him?'

'Maybe.' Eaton bent to get a closer look. When she saw his face, her eyes narrowed. 'Huh.'

'What?' Anya asked.

'I've seen him before. You said this is your father?'

'Yes. Where did you see him?'

'Never mind that now. Help me roll him over. *Don't* touch his hand, or anything wet.' Eaton sniffed the air. 'That's etorphine hydrochloride. It can penetrate skin. If you get any on you, you'll pass out too.'

The three of them gingerly rolled Scanner onto his side. Eaton pressed a finger to his neck. 'Strong pulse. But if we don't get him out of town before the warhead is dropped, he'll die—just like the rest of us. I'll grab his legs. You two take his arms.'

They lifted Scanner. He didn't seem so heavy at first. But after a minute of carrying him towards the exit, Jarli could already tell that they would get exhausted quickly.

'We can't leave Plowman,' he said. 'Not if the warhead—'

'It's not safe to take him with us,' Eaton said. 'We have to stop Fisher from dropping the bomb.'

Plowman's yells and protests faded as they moved away from the cell block, through the corridors of the prison. Eaton stopped at an intersection.

'I don't want to go outside,' she said. 'Plowman's drones are still circling the town. I don't know exactly what he's programmed them to do.'

'Oh, and I just remembered,' Anya said. 'The robot is out there.'

'What?'

'It fell out the window when it was chasing me.'

Jarli stared. 'And it's still operational?'

'Yes. It is pacing right outside the door. If we go out there, it will stun us.'

Jarli's heart sank. Scanner's body felt heavier than ever. 'And there's no other way out. Viper sealed the hole in the wall.'

'Yes, but Viper made some other renovations,' Eaton said. 'This way.'

'Finally.' Bess lifted a magazine off the shelf. It was wrapped in dusty plastic, like all the other publications in the compactor.

The compactor filled the whole archive room—a row of metal bookcases, all mounted on wheels and tracks so they could be pushed together to save space. Bess had been fascinated at first, but an hour of searching in it had dulled her enthusiasm.

'The May issue?' the librarian asked.

'From five years ago. Right.'

The librarian reached for it, but Bess held it back. 'I just need to take a quick look,' she said. 'Before you start digitising.'

'You are trying my patience, young lady,' the librarian warned.

Bess was already taking off the plastic. 'It'll take five seconds,' she promised. She didn't say what she was thinking—that maybe the librarian was the one who had deleted the record. Maybe he was involved in the conspiracy. Whatever was in here, she had to see it before he had a chance to erase it.

She opened the magazine and started scanning through, hoping she would spot the word 'Viper' before the librarian took it away. It must be in here somewhere. The computer said so. And why would Viper have deleted the record if it wasn't about him?

Bess was halfway through the magazine when a different word caught her eye. MALBURSE. Hadn't the defence minister gotten in some kind of trouble over a place called Malburse? The same minister Viper had tried to kill?

Bess stopped skimming and started reading properly. Her eyes grew wider and wider.

'That's more than five seconds,' the librarian said. 'Give it here.'

Bess barely heard him. Parts of the story she already knew—there was a small village on the other side of the world, in a war-torn region called Malburse. A local had leaked information about enemy combatants using the village to stockpile weapons. Aaron Fisher, the Minister for Defence, had discovered that this source was unreliable, but sent troops into the village anyway. It turned out to be a trap. His soldiers died, along with many civilians. Fisher had kept his job by blaming the assistant minister for everything. The assistant was forced to resign.

The only part Bess hadn't seen before was the list of casualties. She read the last name and felt the floor open up beneath her.

VETERANS MONTHLY MAY ISSUE

Mourning at Malburse

(*continued from page 23*) . . .

and the assistant minister has since resigned. The families of those who gave their lives in the botched raid declined to make a statement.

MALBURSE CASUALTY RECORD

David **'Nursing Home'** *Simms (deceased)*

Tak **'Huntsman'** *Lee (deceased)*

Kelsey **'Diamond'** *Rose (deceased)*

Harry **'Smooth'** *Crudup (deceased)*

Maria **'Viper'** *Eaton (wounded)*

PAGE 24

DOWN INTO THE LABYRINTH

'How did you find this?' Jarli asked, staring down into the tunnel.

Eaton avoided the question. 'Help me get him down the ladder,' she said, grabbing Scanner's collar.

The steel trapdoor had been hidden under a battered filing cabinet in one of the ground-floor offices. Underneath was a dark pit. Eaton said it led to the labyrinth of coal mining tunnels beneath Kelton. They could make their way beneath the school, under the lake at the bottom of the falls, and then to a sewer grate near Eaton's apartment.

When she said this, Jarli realised how exhausted he was. He had been up all night. It was 7 a.m. Only five hours until Viper's deadline. Four until Fisher would drop a thermobaric bomb on the town. Every distant sound made Jarli flinch.

The smell of dirt and stone brought back bad memories. A year ago, he and Anya had been trapped in this maze of tunnels for a while. Anyone who got lost down here would die of thirst before they found their way out.

Jarli swallowed his discomfort and climbed down the ladder, holding up one of Scanner's arms. Anya climbed beside him, carrying the other, while Eaton hefted his legs from below.

Soon they were in the TUNNEL. It was so much colder down here. The floor was rough and sloped downward. The walls were jagged, the low ceiling held up by ancient wooden beams. They shuffled downhill, carrying Scanner.

Jarli noticed a lump of yellow clay, apparently glued to the ceiling. Black lines were threaded across it, like cheese wire.

'Uh, you see that?' Jarli asked Anya.

Anya looked up, and paled. 'Miss Eaton? There is a demolition charge attached to the roof.'

Eaton glanced at it. 'Looks like a way to collapse the tunnel in an emergency.'

'Left over from the mining days?'

'No. Viper must have placed it there as a security measure.'

Jarli felt a stab of panic. 'So we could get buried alive in here?'

'If it goes off. We should keep moving.'

'How long will it take to get to your car?' Jarli asked, following her.

'We're not going far,' Eaton promised.

'Plowman is trapped,' Anya said, grunting under Scanner's weight. 'That means he cannot release the toxin. Therefore we only have to worry about the warhead. Correct?'

'No. The botulism will be dispersed over the town either way.'

'Why?'

'Plowman is a brilliant roboticist,' Eaton said carefully. 'He's more than capable of setting up an automatic dispersal device. Right, Jarli?'

Jarli nodded. 'He would have loaded it onto one of his drones so it could cover the whole town with particles. You saw the size of that crashed drone—it could easily carry the canister. He probably programmed one before he gave himself the surgery.'

Anya looked perplexed. 'He performed the surgery upon himself? Did he break his own arm, too?'

It did sound unlikely when she said it out loud. *But,* thought Jarli, *what other explanation was there?*

'He used an autonomous robot to do the surgery,' he told Anya. 'Like Miss Eaton said, he's brilliant.'

'But why would he want to destroy Kelton? It does not make sense.'

'Bess and I were working on a theory,' Jarli said. 'We thought maybe Viper was an ex-soldier.'

'Why?'

'Because he tried to kill Aaron Fisher, the Minister

for Defence. And because he had burns all over his face. We thought he might have been wounded on the battlefield because of something the minister did, and wanted revenge. But Plowman was never a soldier, and the theory doesn't explain why he would want to destroy Kelton.'

'I guess you were wrong,' Eaton said casually.

Jarli's phone beeped. LIE

Anya and Jarli exchanged a glance.

'You *don't* think I was wrong?' Jarli asked.

Eaton turned away. 'Well, it sounded like a good theory. But like you say, Plowman was never a soldier.'

'You were, though,' Jarli said.

'I was a surgeon in the army,' Eaton said. 'Not a soldier. I treated a lot of people with burns like that, but I never crossed paths with Plowman.'

For a moment, the only sound was the shuffling of their footsteps on the tunnel floor.

Then Scanner muttered something.

'Dad!' Anya cried.

They lowered him to the ground. Scanner's eyes were open, but they were rolling wildly, like he was still dreaming. His brow was beaded with sweat, despite the cold.

'Dad! Can you hear me?'

'Sophia?' Scanner's voice cracked. He spoke

slowly, like he was still half in a dream.

Anya touched his face. 'No, Dad, it is me. Anya.'

Jarli's phone rang. He was going to ignore it, but then he realised it could be his Dad, or Doug.

It wasn't. When he pulled the phone out of his pocket, a picture of Bess was glowing on the screen.

Jarli answered the phone and put it to his ear.

'Jarli,' Bess said. 'Where are you?'

'I'm in the old tunnels. Why?'

'Are you alone?'

'No. I—'

At that moment, Scanner's eyes finally focused . . . on Eaton.

'You,' he said. 'You're the doctor who put the chip in me.'

'It's Eaton,' Bess said urgently. 'Can you hear me, Jarli? Eaton is Viper!'

Jarli turned to look at Eaton.

She was already pointing a gun at them.

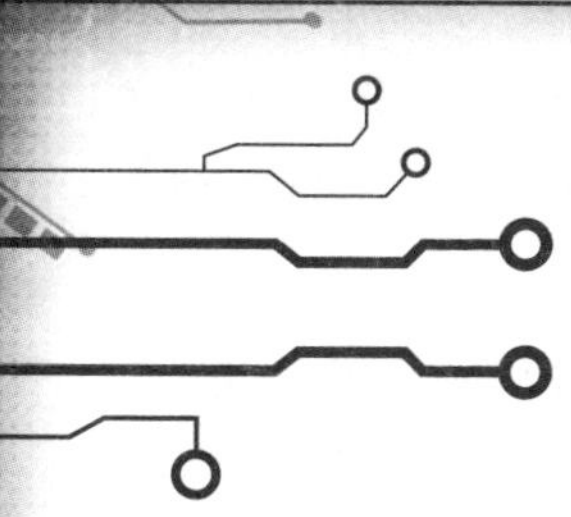

FETCH

Jarli stared at the gun. It was a compact pistol, but even so, he didn't know where she had been hiding it. He felt dizzy.

'Miss Eaton!' Anya sounded aghast. 'What are you doing?'

'Keep your distance,' Eaton said, backing away.

'You work for Viper?!'

'No.'

Jarli's phone didn't beep. Eaton's statement was technically true. Jarli was starting to realise that many of Eaton's statements were only technically true.

Bess was still on the phone. 'Oh, no! Is Eaton there? Jarli, *get away from her*. She's Viper!'

'She's Viper,' Jarli repeated, numbly.

Anya's mouth fell open.

Eaton levelled the gun at Jarli. 'Hang up. Put the phone away.'

Jarli pretended to push the end-call button. He dropped the phone into his pocket. Hopefully Bess could still hear everything, although he didn't think that would save them.

'I knew someone would figure it out eventually,' Eaton said. 'I should have guessed it would be you. Back off.' She swivelled the gun towards Anya, who had been slowly creeping up on her.

Anya stopped, and put her hands up.

It all fit. Giving someone a new face wouldn't be too different to repairing an injured one. With the right equipment, removing a memory from somebody's brain might be even easier than removing a bullet. And after seeing all those soldiers die unnecessarily, holding a grudge against the selfish and incompetent defence minister made sense.

It had been Eaton who first told Jarli that Viper was a man with a scarred face, leading him off-track. And every time Viper was up to something, she had always seemed to be nearby.

Jarli remembered how she had turned up at Kelton's hospital with a bunch of flowers, only to find it surrounded by police. *Just visiting a friend,* she'd said. At the time, Jarli's phone had said she was lying—because she was really there to remotely control the surgical robot inside.

Eaton had no expertise with robots, as far as Jarli knew. But he remembered what she had said to Plowman, back at her apartment:

We've met before. You helped me with a technology problem. You don't remember?

Plowman had built her robots for her. Then she had erased his memory of it.

And Jarli's, too.

'We trusted you,' Jarli said, sickened.

'And I let you live,' Eaton said. 'Several times it would have been easier to kill you all, but I didn't. You're welcome.' She glanced down at Scanner, who still seemed to be unable to get up. 'If I'd known that my head of security was secretly helping you, I might have made a different call.'

The last year was racing through Jarli's head, like a video played at 32x speed. At school, Eaton had given him and Bess a way to escape from some bad guys . . . who turned out to be good guys. She had helped him and Anya sneak into the hospital . . . to stop the police from filling it with gas.

'Every time I thought you were helping us,' Jarli said, 'you were really helping yourself.'

'I'm not interested in having this discussion.' Eaton pulled her phone out of her pocket.

'You told me that Plowman was Viper,' Jarli said. 'Why didn't my app go off?'

'I never said that.' Eaton operated her phone without taking her eyes off Jarli and Anya. 'You made up your own mind.'

Jarli thought back to their conversation. It was true—Eaton hadn't told him Plowman was Viper. She had only led him to that conclusion: *Viper is brilliant. Rich. Good with computers and robots. Anti-government. Seems to know everything. Does that sound familiar?*

'But why destroy Kelton?' Jarli asked. 'What did we ever do to you?'

'Nothing,' Viper said. 'That's why I warned everybody to leave.'

'But—'

Suddenly Scanner rolled over and scrambled towards Viper's legs. He somehow had a KNIFE in his hand. Viper jumped back, startled.

Jarli's mind was racing. Scanner must have recovered from the anaesthetic. But he had been hiding it for the last few minutes, waiting for an opportunity to strike.

He hadn't waited long enough.

Viper pushed a button on her phone.

'Argh!' Scanner dropped the knife and clutched his hand. Something was glowing orange under his skin.

'No!' Jarli cried.

'Dad!' Anya screamed.

Scanner started shaking all over. Foamy drool leaked from his mouth.

Viper had activated the poison capsule.

Anya launched herself at Viper with a flying kick. Viper ducked aside, and Anya crashed into the wall.

'Listen to me, Anya!' Viper shouted. 'The snake venom has entered your father's bloodstream. He's dying.'

Jarli had seen this before. Viper had killed a corrupt cop right in front of him, using the same method. Once the capsule had been activated, the cop had died in minutes.

Anya swung a wild fist at Viper's face. Viper stepped back out of range, and levelled the gun at her.

'But you can save his life,' she said.

Anya froze. Jarli held his breath.

Viper pocketed her phone and pulled out a capped syringe. 'This antivenom will save your father—if he gets it in time.'

Anya looked from the syringe to the gun and back. 'What do you want?' she asked coldly.

'Fetch,' Viper said.

She threw the syringe over Anya's shoulder. Jarli jumped sideways, trying to catch it. He missed, and the syringe flew past him, disappearing into the darkness of the tunnel. He heard it bounce once, twice, and then silence.

By the time he looked back at Viper, she was

already running the other way, deeper into the coal mine.

Jarli and Anya sprinted towards where they had heard the syringe land. Jarli hoped it wasn't broken. The antivenom inside was their only hope of saving Scanner's life. There wouldn't be time to get him to the hospital, which would have been evacuated anyway.

Jarli used the torch app on his phone, illuminating the rough floor. Anya was doing the same.

'Where is it?' she demanded. 'Do you see it?'

Something glinted over near the wall. 'There!' Jarli yelled. He snatched up the syringe and tossed it to Anya.

Anya sprinted back to her fallen father. Jarli followed and crouched down next to her.

'I can do this.' Anya uncapped the syringe. 'He trained me for it. You chase Viper. Do not let her get away.'

The fury in her voice was frightening.

'I'm on it,' Jarli said, and he took off after Eaton.

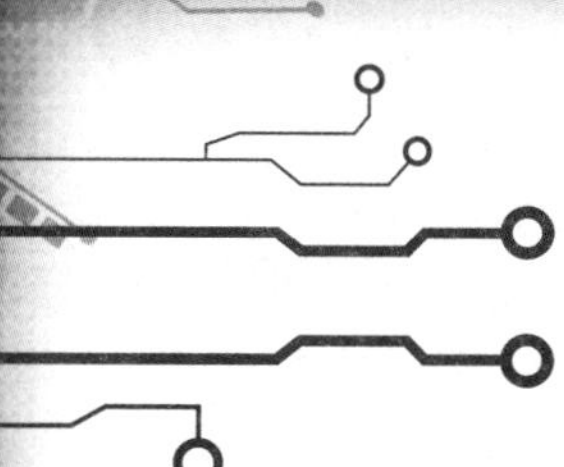

TEN SECONDS TO COMPLY

Jarli ran through the darkness, keeping his head down to avoid the low beams holding up the ceiling. The tunnel twisted and turned, sometimes doubling back on itself like a tangled pile of rope on a boat, slowing him down. And he couldn't see Eaton up ahead, nor hear her footsteps.

Maybe that was a good thing. She had a gun, and probably other tricks up her sleeve. Jarli had nothing except his phone. What was he supposed to do if he caught her?

But if he didn't, she would destroy the town. The place he'd lived his whole life. His only hope was to follow Viper to wherever the botulism canister was hidden, disable it somehow, and contact someone from the government to tell them, all in less than four hours. They wouldn't drop a thermobaric bomb on the town if the botulism was already taken care of . . . would they?

It didn't seem like much of a plan. Jarli kept running, trying to breathe quietly so he could hear

Viper, and so she wouldn't hear him.

He suddenly realised Bess was still on the phone. He took it out of his pocket and pressed it to his ear.

'Bess,' he whispered. 'Anya is trying to save Scanner's life. I'm going after Eaton.'

'What?! Why?'

It was a good question. 'Because if I don't, she'll destroy the town. Or Fisher will drop a thermobaric warhead on it. That's what Scanner said.'

'That's insane. Jarli, you have to get out of there.'

'I can't! I'm the only one who can stop her.'

'Call the police. Or the media, if you don't trust the cops. Dana Reynolds.'

'The cops will never find the botulism in time. But I can follow her right to it. I hope.'

'Jarli—'

'I don't have time for this.' An unexpected tear stung the corner of Jarli's eye. He and Bess never argued. '*You* call the police. Please. Tell them what we know. And then call Reynolds. The world needs to know the truth. She can expose Viper, and maybe stop Fisher from dropping the warhead.'

'Your life is more important than the truth,' Bess insisted.

'Viper might try to kill us to keep her secret. If everyone knows who she is, she might not bother.'

It didn't feel like much of a plan—hoping the

criminal mastermind 'wouldn't bother' killing them. But it was the best he could do.

'Fine,' Bess said. 'I'll call the police, and Reynolds. But you have to get out of there.'

'Tell my Dad—tell my family I love them,' Jarli said. 'And . . . I love you, too. You know that, right?'

'Well, duh.'

Jarli hung up, before the goodbyes could get out of hand.

He suddenly realised he couldn't hear Viper anymore. Maybe he'd already lost her. Maybe Kelton was DOOMED. He kept running, because it was his only hope.

Then he came to a fork in the tunnel. Had Viper gone right or left? There was no way to tell. Fifty-fifty chance. Jarli went right.

Soon there was another fork. Twenty-five, twenty-five. His odds of catching up to her were getting worse and worse. And then:

'I can hear you following me.'

Viper's voice echoed through the gloom, from a long way away. Jarli bit his lip. Had it come from the tunnel on the left or the right?

'Go back,' Viper shouted, 'or you will die. Check your app—am I lying?'

Jarli's phone didn't beep. But he clung to the hope that she was bluffing. She didn't know he was there. Not for sure.

'You have ten seconds to comply.'

Jarli kept scanning the shadows.

'Nine.'

She couldn't shoot him if she couldn't see him.

'Eight.'

The passageway was tight and narrow. She'd have to get close to have a clear line of sight.

'Seven.'

Still impossible to tell where her voice was coming from.

'Six.'

Left, or right? Or behind him somehow?

'Five.'

Jarli pressed himself into a shallow nook in the wall.

'Four.'

Not much of a hiding place.

'Three.'

Her voice seemed to be getting further away, rather than closer.

'Two.'

Quieter and quieter. Had she overlooked him, and gone the wrong way?

And then, in the deepest distance:

'One.'

Silence fell.

Jarli listened, his heart pounding, sweat gluing his hair to his forehead. There were no gunshots, no footsteps, no more voices.

Eaton must have been bluffing. She had tricked him into hiding while she ran away, getting so far ahead of him that he would never catch up.

Or maybe there was something he hadn't thought of. Perhaps she planned to kill him from a distance—

Boom. The noise of the blast came from a long way away, but it still made Jarli flinch. Was Eaton trying to blow him up? If so, she had planted the bomb in the wrong place.

She could be collapsing the tunnel so he couldn't follow her. Trapping him down here in the dark. The thought was like ice in Jarli's veins. *Don't panic,* he told himself.

A second explosion rang out, equally far away. Jarli felt like a submarine, hiding at the bottom of the ocean while a battleship dropped depth charges from above.

But the echoes of the second explosion didn't fade like the first one. Instead they seemed to be growing louder. Closer. A distant hiss became a rumble and then a roar, like a wave approaching the beach.

Suddenly Jarli realised what was going on. At the bottom of Kelton Falls was a lake. Eaton had told him that one of the tunnels went right under it.

Now she had detonated a demolition charge in that tunnel, destroying the ceiling and unleashing all that water.

She was going to drown him.

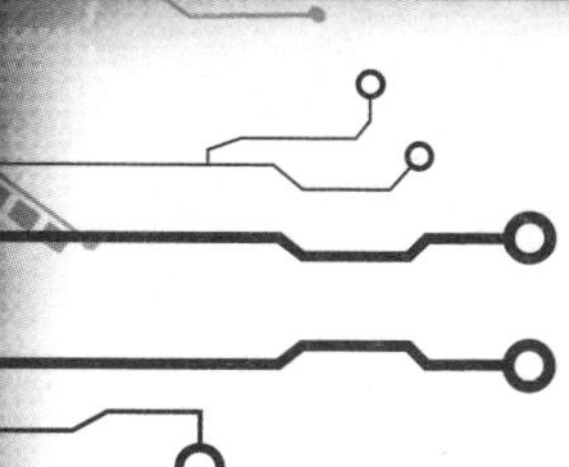

JAGGED STONE WALLS

'Anya!' Jarli screamed, hoping she could hear him. 'The tunnel's flooding! Run!' He sprinted back the way he had come. He could hear the water rushing through the tunnel towards him, splashing against the walls, the tight turns driving the current.

The rain had been constant over the last two weeks. It was still raining now. The lake would be full. There was more than enough water to drown him in these narrow tunnels.

Jarli reached the fork and swerved. Kept running. A few twists in the tunnel later, he realised he'd turned the wrong way. It was too late to go back. When he looked over his shoulder, he saw that the flood was already here. Ankle-deep water raced towards him, white at the edges where the jagged stone walls had churned it up. It wouldn't stay ankle-deep for long.

And worse, Jarli was running downhill again. If he hit a dead end, or if there was more water ahead of him, he was doomed. That wrong turn might have killed him.

Cold water sloshed against Jarli's calf muscles. His shoes were instantly soaked. The extra weight slowed him down. He splashed clumsily along the tunnel, looking for a way out.

As he rounded a corner, he found himself on a slight uphill slope. But that only slowed him down even more, and the water level was rising faster than the path. Soon Jarli was wading through knee-deep water. In no time at all, it was up to his hips. The roaring of the water behind him was deafening. It was so cold. If he didn't drown, he might freeze to death.

Jarli's torchlight glinted off something shiny up ahead. *More water!* He was doomed.

No—it was something made of metal. A ladder. Jarli half-ran, half-swam towards it.

The water was chest-high now, pushing against his back. The current made it hard to stop his feet slipping out from under him. If he lost his footing, he would be swept away and PULVERISED against the walls.

The ladder was coming up on his right. Jarli pocketed his phone and struggled through the flood towards it. The water was at his neck now, tickling his chin. When he had almost reached the ladder, the current became too strong, pushing him off his feet.

'No!' He flung out a desperate hand, barely snagging the side of the ladder in his slippery fingers. The full force of the water hit him now. He gripped the ladder with both hands as his head went under, and the current blasted his body sideways like a flag in a strong wind. He dragged himself up to the next rung, and then the next. With every metre he went up, he expected to find air, but there was none. His lungs were bursting. He was blinded by the water and the darkness. He couldn't hear anything other than the smashing of waves on walls.

One more rung and his head was finally above the rushing water. He took in a deep breath and kept climbing.

The water pulled at his legs, trying to suck him back down into the tunnel. Jarli had the surreal—and disgusting—feeling that he was being flushed down a toilet. He finally reached the top of the ladder and dragged himself up over the edge, out of the water and onto a gritty concrete floor. He lay there for a moment, shivering.

When he looked back down, the water had reached the top of the ladder. The flow was only getting stronger. He guessed it would take a long time for the lake to drain completely.

Jarli looked around. It was pitch black in here.

Where was he?

He dug his phone out of his pocket. The case seemed to have protected it from the water. He shook the droplets off and shone the light around. On one side of the chamber were two old metal doors, sealed with shiny new padlocks. An unlit hurricane lamp dangled from the wall between them. On the other side of the room was a vent, leading to a tiny crawlspace. Suddenly Jarli realised he had been here before. The vent was connected to Eaton's office, at school. The hole Jarli had crawled out of hadn't been there before, though. It was new.

Viper made some other renovations, Eaton had said.

One of the two doors led back down to the old mining tunnels. Eaton had taken him through there once, 'helping' him escape from the police.

He had never been through the other door. And now he saw that the gleaming padlock on it had been left open.

Jarli stepped forward cautiously. Why would Eaton leave the door unlocked? Maybe she had cleared out whatever was inside. Or she was so close to her endgame that she didn't care if anyone found her stuff.

Or maybe she was inside.

Jarli edged closer and closer to the door. There

was no handle—just flat metal. He pushed, and the door swung open with a creak that made him wince.

It was darker still within. No sound of movement, but it was hard to hear over the distant thunder and the water rushing through the tunnels.

Jarli's phone battery was down to thirty-one per cent. He wasn't willing to fumble around in the dark, especially if Eaton might be waiting in yet another trap, so he lifted the hurricane lamp off the wall. He'd never used one before, but there was only one button. He pushed it, and after a few seconds of clicking, the spark ignited the kerosene. A warm yellow glow illuminated the darkness of the room beyond.

BLACK TIDE

It sounded like an oncoming train. A rumbling and hissing, magnified by the walls of the tunnel. Getting louder and louder, so Anya barely heard Jarli's warning: 'Anya! The tunnel's flooding! Run!'

She grabbed her father's shoulders. 'Dad! We have to move.'

He didn't stir. She had injected him with the antivenom only a couple of minutes ago. He hadn't regained consciousness yet.

The robot's anaesthetic could have slowed down his recovery. Or maybe this was another one of Viper's tricks. The antivenom might have been fake. Perhaps her father was already—

No. She wouldn't let herself even think the word.

Anya peered into the darkness of the tunnel. She couldn't see the water yet, but she could hear it. Any second now, this tunnel was going to be flooded.

'Dad.' She searched his face for a reaction. 'Wake up!'

His eyelids fluttered.

The approaching water was too loud to say anything else. Anya grabbed her father under his arms and started dragging him up the tunnel, back towards the prison.

He had been heavy even when she had Jarli and Eaton's help. Now he seemed to weigh a tonne, but the adrenaline gave her strength. She moved as fast as she could, but the water was faster. Soon she could see it up the end of the tunnel. Then it was lapping at her father's feet. Not long after that it was washing over her own ankles, as cold as ice.

The flood actually helped her pull him along—he half-floated on the black tide. But this made it harder for her to walk. The gritty water sloshed around her legs as she dragged him. She felt like she was wearing concrete shoes.

As she turned a corner, the ladder back up to the prison came into view. If she could just get to it, maybe she could haul her father up to safety.

'Almost there, Dad,' she muttered. 'Come on. We can do this.'

She struggled to keep his head above the water as she waded backwards through the flow. He was unconscious—if his face went under, he would drown. The water was already up to her hips. She hugged his chest from behind, desperate to hold him up.

Anya reached the ladder. Grabbed a rung. She tried to drag her father up, but he was too heavy. The current was getting stronger, tugging him back.

'No!' she shouted. The water rushed over her shoulders. She wasn't strong enough to pull her father up. His chin dipped beneath the surface.

Anya gasped in a lungful of air and let her own head go under. She grabbed a lower rung with one hand and tried to push her father up from underneath. She couldn't see anything in the blackness. His weight was crushing—

And when she tried to adjust her grip on him, he slipped. His weight shifted off her, and suddenly her hand was empty.

Anya screamed underwater, a stream of bubbles exploding from her mouth before they were sucked away by the current. Gripping the ladder with one hand, she thrashed around with the other, trying to grab her father.

Her fingers found only water.

He was gone.

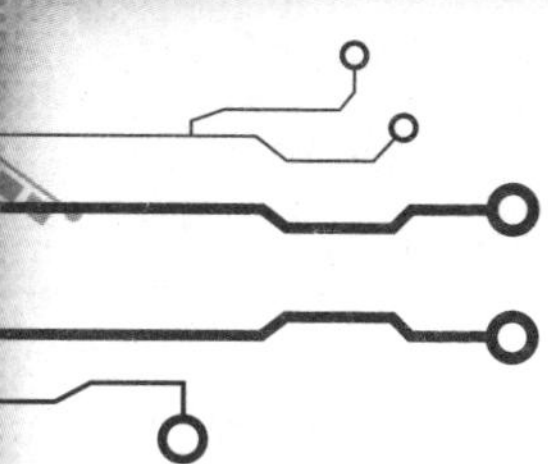

THE SNAKE'S LAIR

Eaton wasn't there.

Instead, Jarli found himself in a long, narrow workshop with a polished wooden floor. Lined up along the left-hand wall was a sink, a bank of car batteries, a fire blanket and extinguisher, an air conditioner, a giant freezer and some metal shelves topped with jars. One of the jars was labelled **SULPHURIC ACID.** Another was labelled **VENOM: INLAND TAIPAN.**

Along the other wall was a stainless steel workbench and a wheeled chair. Light bulbs dangled from chains on the ceiling, but when Jarli found the switch and flicked it, nothing happened. No power.

Jarli took a moment to orient himself. If Eaton's office was behind him, then the rest of the school gymnasium would be to his left. Eaton must have secretly walled off a small portion of it during the school holidays or something, and no-one had even noticed. That explained why the gym was so hot, even at night. When the air conditioner cooled this workshop, it would pump the leftover heat into the gym.

Jarli ran over to the freezer and opened it, hoping to find the botulism canister. But the freezer was empty except for a slowly melting crust of ice. The canister might have been in here, but not anymore.

A journal rested on the workbench. Jarli opened it up, looking for clues about where Viper might have hidden the toxin. He flicked through page after page of notes about Aaron Fisher. Eaton had chronicled every detail of his long career, highlighting every alleged crime. But there was nothing about the botulism, and nothing about Viper herself.

Above the workbench, a map was tacked to the wall. Jarli held up the hurricane lamp for a better look. It was a map of the whole country, straight lines crisscrossing all over it. A column of times and dates were scrawled on the right-hand side.

All the lines passed through Kelton. As though this town was the epicentre of something.

Jarli frowned, trying to work out what he was looking at. Had Viper been measuring the distance between Kelton and other cities? Why?

Then it hit him. These were flight paths. Viper had marked all the flights which passed over Kelton, and noted the times they would be right above it.

There was also a diagram of a small passenger plane, with some parts highlighted and notes scribbled around them. Jarli was no expert, but it looked like Viper had been studying the air-filtration system.

Maybe this was old stuff from when she crashed a plane into Doug's house. But no. Jarli checked the dates, and saw that the flights on the map were more recent than that.

He remembered that after the plane hit Doug's house, Viper had tried to steal another RCG—an electromagnetic device designed to disrupt aircraft systems. She had failed, but the attempt proved that she had a second target.

The defence minister. She had tried to kill him when he visited Kelton for a conference. Now she was waiting for him to fly overhead so she could try again.

Why destroy Kelton? What did we ever do to you?

Nothing. That's why I warned everybody to leave.

The whole jigsaw snapped together in Jarli's head. Viper was going to disperse the botulism in the air above Kelton. The cloud would make the town uninhabitable—and the minister's plane would fly right through it. Would the toxin leak into the plane's cabin? Viper must think so, after studying the air-filtration system. If she was right, the minister would die. So would the pilot, and anyone else on the plane.

For Viper's plan to work, a drone would have to release the toxic particles *above* the plane. Probably too high to see. Jarli's heart sank. It could be up there already, with the canister, beyond the reach of all the people searching for it. But the drone would respond to signals from the ground—maybe it could be hacked.

There was another door at the back of the room. It was just wood, but the rubber draft-stoppers around it made Jarli think it might be airtight. He reached for the brass handle, and then paused.

It would make sense to put the botulism in an airtight room. If Jarli opened the door, he might expose himself to the toxin. But there was no time to find safety gear, and he had to know for sure. He twisted the handle.

Inside was a tiny hospital room. There was a monitor, a mini fridge and a tray with surgical tools lined up under a UV lamp. The tools were wickedly sharp. One had **BONE SAW** inscribed on it. Another was labelled **TOOTHED FORCEPS.** One device, which looked like a vacuum cleaner crossed with a hole punch, was called the **AIR DERMATOME.**

And there was a bed. With a body.

Covered by a sheet.

Jarli froze. This was where Viper did her surgeries. Where she gave new faces to criminals. Maybe it was where she had taken Jarli's memories, too.

He stayed perfectly still until he was sure the sheet wasn't moving. Whoever was under there, they weren't breathing.

Jarli didn't want to look. He had seen a dead body once before—the cop that Viper had poisoned. There had been no blood or anything, but the sight had given him NIGHTMARES, even after he talked it over with the gentle-voiced police therapist.

If Viper was planning to replace someone else, Jarli told himself, *I need to know who.*

He swallowed. Peeled back the sheet—

And screamed.

He was looking at his own face. Eyes closed, lips slightly parted, like Sleeping Beauty.

Viper had been planning to replace *him*.

UNNATURAL GROWL

'Mr Plowman?' Anya called.

She was still drenched with icy water, but she barely felt it. She was on autopilot—she wasn't even sure how she'd gotten here, back inside Throwaway, standing in front of Plowman's cell. Her mind was still down there, in the cold, dark water, with her dad.

He was gone. And if she had been stronger, he would still be alive.

Plowman didn't seem to hear her. He sat cross-legged in his cell, facing the wall. She couldn't see his face.

There was a green button on the wall a few metres away from the cage door. Anya pushed it, and the lock clicked.

Plowman whirled around. 'Don't let me out!' His voice was an unnatural growl.

'We need to get out of here,' Anya's autopilot said. 'Before the warhead is dropped. The tunnels are flooded. You are the only one who can deal with the robot guarding the door.'

'Listen to me,' Plowman said. His eyes were red-rimmed, and his knuckles were bleeding. 'You can't let me out. I'm Viper.'

Eaton's cleverness was sickening. She hadn't only convinced Jarli that Plowman was guilty. She had also convinced Plowman himself.

'You are not Viper,' Anya heard herself say.

'I didn't want to believe it either. But it's true.'

'Eaton is Viper.'

Plowman looked at her for a moment, then shook his head. 'That doesn't make sense.'

'Get up.'

Plowman did. He opened the cage door a crack and closed it again, locking himself in. Then he sat back down.

A ball of rage ignited in Anya's gut. It was like a power surge, overloading her autopilot.

'Get up!' she screamed.

Plowman didn't. He bowed his head, as though waiting for an executioner's axe.

'You think it has to be you?' Anya continued. 'You think you are the only one smart enough to be Viper? Understanding computers does not make you a genius. My father was more intelligent than you—he lived a double life for years, always risking his safety, never making a mistake—and Eaton still fooled him. Now he's dead.'

At that, Plowman looked up.

'She might have killed Jarli, too.' Anya pushed the button again. 'If you're so smart, get us out of here. I need to tell my mother that her husband is gone.'

Plowman watched her for a long moment. 'I'm sorry,' he said finally.

'Don't give me sorry,' Anya snapped. 'Give me a way out of here.'

'I don't have one. I don't know how to get rid of the robot.'

'Then what use are you?' Anya shouted, and kicked the bars of the cage. She threw her wet, useless phone at Plowman. He ducked, and it smashed against the wall.

'Give me *your* phone,' she demanded. 'So I can call an actual genius.'

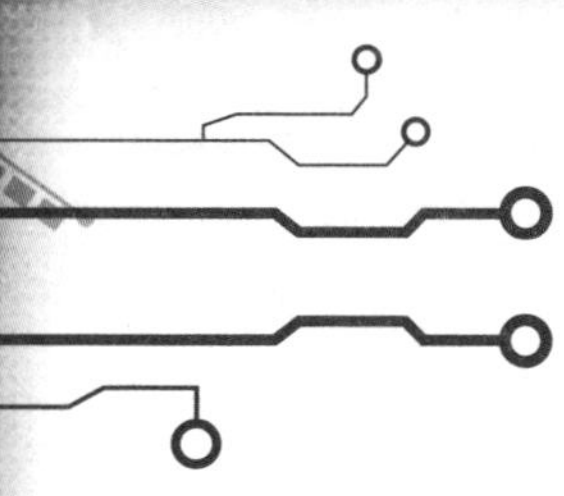

UNKNOWN NUMBER

Jarli woke to the sound of his phone ringing.

When the world stopped spinning, he realised he was on the floor of Viper's workshop. He sneezed out a cloud of dust. How had he gotten here?

He rolled over, woozily. He remembered seeing himself—or someone who had been surgically altered to look like him—on the operating table. He must have walked out of the room, although he didn't remember doing that. And then what? Fainted?

He checked the phone screen. Plowman. He answered. 'Hello?'

'Jarli.' It was Anya's voice. 'I'm with Plowman. We need your help.'

'Anya.' A wave of relief hit Jarli. 'I'm glad you're OK.'

'We are back at the prison.' Anya sounded strangely flat. 'The tunnels are flooded, so we need to get past the robot somehow.'

Jarli rubbed his eyes as his brain kicked into gear. 'It's still guarding the door?'

'I am looking out the window right now. It is still there.'

'Have you got anything you could use to make another EMP?'

'We have nothing. And remember, the EMP did not work on the robot last time.'

'Oh. Right.' Jarli frowned at the workbench, not really seeing it. He turned the problem over in his mind, examining all the angles. Anya and Plowman didn't really have *nothing*—they had a phone, and clothes, and a filing cabinet, and the prison itself. But Jarli couldn't think of a way to use any of that to deal with the robot. So he had to find some extra equipment and give it to them. But the robot would stop him from approaching the building.

Tricky.

'Can Plowman control his drones from there?' he asked suddenly.

'I am not sure. I will put him on.'

Plowman came on the line. 'Jarli.'

Jarli suddenly remembered that he had locked Plowman in a cell.

'Uh, hi, Mr Plowman,' he said awkwardly.

Silence hissed in his ear.

'I'm sorry,' Jarli said. 'I should have trusted you.'

Plowman just grunted.

Jarli cleared his throat. 'I'm gonna get you and

Anya out of there, OK?'

'OK.' Plowman didn't sound like he cared one way or the other. Viper had really messed with his head.

'I'm going to make something that will help you deal with the robot. But I need a way to get it to you. If I text you an address, can you get one of your drones to pick it up and deliver it to you?'

'I suppose,' Plowman said slowly. 'What is it?'

'I don't know yet. Give me a sec.'

Jarli ended the call, and started looking around Viper's workshop for something he could use. There was a fire blanket. Anya and Plowman might be able to hide under it as they crawled out the door. But Jarli wasn't sure how the robot would react. He needed to know more about it.

His phone started ringing again. Unknown number.

Viper, Jarli thought, though he had no reason to think so. After holding the phone like a live grenade for a second, he answered: 'Who is this?'

'Jarli?'

Now that he heard his real father's voice, he wondered how he could ever have fallen for Cobra's impersonation. His eyes filled with tears. 'Dad?'

'It's me, Jarli. God, it's so good to hear your voice.'

There was a painful lump in Jarli's throat. 'You too. Where are you?'

'I'm driving, with your friend Doug. We've almost reached Axe Falls. Your school nurse found us and let us out of Viper's prison—'

'The school nurse *was* Viper, Dad.'

'I'm sorry, what?'

Jarli repeated the words. Saying them out loud made them real somehow. The betrayal stung all over again. His anger grew.

'Why did she let us go?' Dad asked, after Jarli had explained everything.

'I don't know. Apparently all the other prisoners were taken away in a transport truck. Maybe she wanted them out of the way before she releases the botulism. I think she's going to drop it from a drone, above the defence minister's flight path.'

Doug came on the line. 'Jarli. Are you there?'

'Doug,' Jarli said. 'I'm so glad you're alive.'

'Yeah, well, I nearly wasn't. I got attacked by a robot. Tell you all about it sometime. But before that, I overheard some guards talking when I was in the prison. One of them said something about a rocket.'

'A rocket?'

'Yeah,' Doug said. 'So maybe she's not using a drone.'

Jarli felt sick. Unlike drones, rockets usually

weren't designed to be controlled from a distance. Jarli wouldn't be able to hack a rocket remotely. His only hope was to get to it before the launch.

'Did you get a close look at the robot?' he asked.

'Way too close. Why?'

'It's got Anya cornered at Throwaway. I'm trying to work out a way to disable it.'

'Oh, no! Uh . . . I didn't see any obvious weaknesses,' Doug said. 'It looked pretty tough, Jarli.'

'Could we block its anaesthetic squirter-thingy somehow?'

'With what?'

'I don't know,' Jarli said. 'Glue?'

'The pressure would just blow it out, no matter what you used,' Doug said. 'And you'd have to be right up in the robot's face to get the glue or chewing gum or whatever into the nozzle. And this thing is *fast*. Even if you succeeded somehow, it'd still be able to zap you with a stun gun.'

'OK, OK.' Jarli sighed. 'It was just an idea.'

'Could you make some kind of EMP device?'

'We tried that. The robot is shielded somehow.'

'In that case,' Doug said, 'go for the eyes. If it can't see Anya, it can't attack her.'

'How many eyes does it have?'

'Six. Wraparound, so it can see in all directions.

But if you chucked a blanket over it, or a bucket of paint, I don't think it would be able to see.'

Jarli wondered how close Anya would have to be for Doug's suggestion to work. It seemed risky—but Doug had given Jarli another idea.

'What if the robot saw Anya,' Jarli said, 'but thought it was seeing Viper?'

'Why would—wait. Does this thing have facial recognition?'

'Plowman thought so. He's there, too. And Scanner.' Jarli realised that he hadn't heard Scanner's voice on the phone when Anya had called him. He hoped the antivenom had worked.

'Hang on,' Doug said. 'Your dad wants to talk to you again.'

Dad's voice came back on the line. 'Where are you, Jarli?'

'I'm at school.'

'What? You're still in Kelton?!'

Jarli swallowed. 'We—'

'You have to get out! The . . . thing, the bacterial weapon, it will be released in less than two hours!'

Jarli didn't tell his father about the WARHEAD. He checked his watch. He was alarmed to see that it was already 10.14 a.m.

'I still have time to stop her,' he said.

'Jarli, listen to me. For once, please just listen.

You need to leave, right now. It's not your job to stop Viper.'

'Someone has to.'

'She might release the toxin early,' Doug said in the background. 'It could happen at any moment.'

'She won't. She can't.' Jarli looked at the map on the wall. 'I figured out her plan, Dad. She's waiting for the defence minister's plane to fly overhead—'

'Jarli.' He could hear his father getting angry. 'You need to leave.'

'But I can save the town.'

'Forget the town,' Dad said. 'I care about *you*. Please, just get out.'

'Don't worry about me, Dad. I'll see you soon.' Jarli ended the call. He sniffed, and wiped his eyes on his sleeve. Then he looked at the map and dialled Bess.

SELLING SILENCE

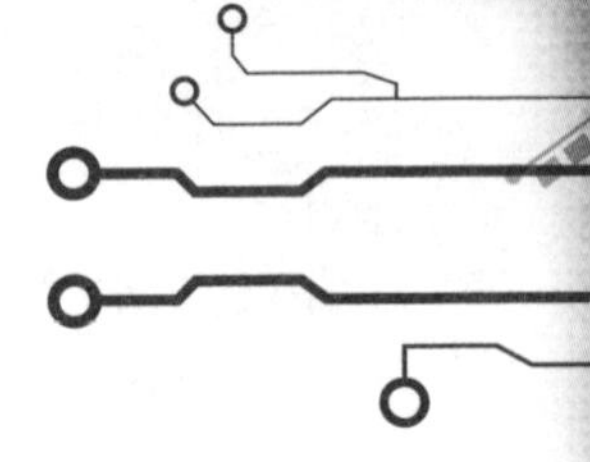

Aaron Fisher sat in the business class lounge, a half-finished macchiato in one hand, watching one of the screens on the wall. He was flying by private jet, so his flight wasn't listed. But the screen helped him keep track of the time.

Other screens had cricket, or news. They played quietly, unlike the TVs blaring at maximum volume downstairs in the economy lounges. There weren't many announcements up here, either. *The business class lounge isn't here to sell gourmet coffee or hot towels*, he reflected. *It sells silence*.

His deputy, Rizvi, was looking at flight paths on her phone. 'We're going to fly right over Kelton,' she said.

'Thirty thousand feet over,' Fisher said, without taking his eyes off the screen. 'Relax. The general tells me the shockwave will be much less, and in any case, the detonation will happen an hour before we get there. It's not nuclear. No fallout.'

'Maybe we should tell the pilot to plan a new

course,' Rizvi said.

'If we take the long way around, that will give the opposition an extra hour to spin this before I land,' Fisher said. 'Honestly, Sandra. You just don't think like a politician.'

Rizvi didn't look as offended as he thought she should.

Her phone rang, disturbing the hush in the lounge. Fisher glared at her as she answered.

'Yes?' She looked alarmed. 'Where did you hear that? . . . It's not our policy to comment on—'

Fisher grabbed the phone. Apparently his deputy had no idea how to kill a story. *No comment* never did the trick.

'Who is this?' he demanded.

'Minister!' He immediately recognised the cheery voice of Dana Reynolds. 'We'll soon be reporting that you're planning to drop a thermobaric warhead on the town of Kelton. Care to comment?'

'I'm planning no such thing,' Fisher lied, wondering how fast he could find and fire whoever had leaked this information.

He heard Reynolds's phone beep. LIE

'Thanks for confirming,' she said smugly. But he could tell from her tone of voice that this conversation wasn't live on air. There was a chance to fix this.

He couldn't blame the explosion on Viper if

Reynolds started reporting it as a military operation ahead of time. He needed a new plan.

'You're referring to one of many options that was presented to me by the assistant minister,' Fisher said, and he saw Rizvi's eyes widen. 'I said it was completely off the table. There will be no bomb—if you report one, you'll wind up looking very foolish indeed. And you can quote me.'

He hung up and tossed the phone to his shocked deputy. 'Call the general,' he told her. 'Tell her to abort the launch. We need another way to stop Viper.'

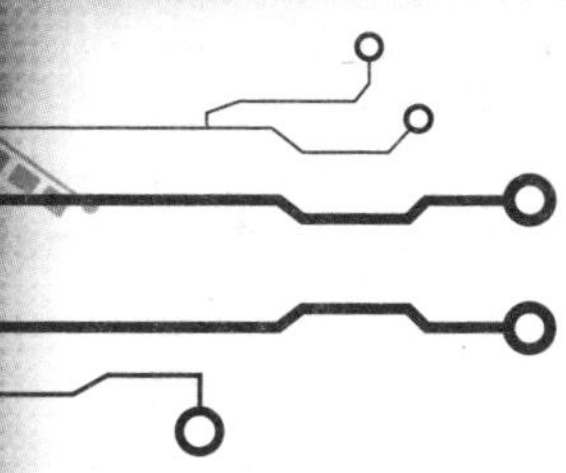

A MASSIVE SECURITY RISK

Bess limped out onto the covered balcony before answering the phone. Her mum, Jarli's mum and Jarli's sister were all in the hotel room behind her, quietly freaking out. She had a feeling that they wouldn't like whatever Jarli was about to say.

She was right.

'Bess,' he said, before she'd even opened her mouth. 'I'm still in Kelton. I'm going to stop Viper, no matter what, and I don't want to hear any guff about saving myself and abandoning the town.'

'Did you say "guff"?' Bess asked.

'It just came to me,' Jarli said. 'So are you going to help, or not?'

Bess glanced back through the glass. Kirstie looked curious, but the two mums were ignoring her.

'I'll help you,' she said. 'Obviously I'll help you. But what can I do from here?'

'OK.' Jarli sounded relieved. 'Firstly, I need to get Anya out of prison.'

'Pardon?'

'I'm about to email you a document. Does the hotel have a printer?'

'I don't know. Probably.'

'Well, I need you to print out the picture, cut it up and bring it outside. One of Plowman's drones will be there to pick it up soon.'

Bess felt like she was dreaming. 'Print a picture, cut it up and wait for a drone to collect it?'

'It's a mask. You'll understand when you see it,' Jarli promised. 'I figured out Viper's plan—she's going to use a rocket to release the botulism into the air above Kelton, so the defence minister will be poisoned when his plane flies through it.'

'Wait. Won't Fisher avoid flying over a town which is about to become uninhabitable?'

Jarli was silent for a moment. 'Probably,' he said finally. 'But Viper's rocket might be long-distance. Fisher wouldn't have to fly right over the town—just within range of it. Anyway, the problem is that I don't know where she's planning to launch the canister from.'

'Right,' Bess said slowly. 'You need me to look up the flight path of the plane? And look for any hilltops or tall buildings under it?'

'No. She left a map behind with the all flight paths marked. I need you to work out which plane the defence minister will be on.'

Bess rubbed her eyes. She'd been up all night. 'How can I find that out? In fact, how would *Viper* find out?'

'I don't know. I'm guessing she has sources we can't access. People she's chipped, who have to do whatever she says.'

Bess watched the rain splattering the street for a minute. Jarli often depended on her to get him out of tough spots. But this wasn't just tough—it was impossible.

'You could call the government, posing as a reporter, or something?' Jarli suggested.

'They wouldn't give that information to a reporter.'

'They might if they were asked in the right way.'

'We could call Dana Reynolds,' Bess said. 'She might have an idea—'

The sliding door opened behind Bess. Kirstie stepped onto the balcony. She closed the door behind her. 'That's Jarli, right?' she said. 'Give it here.'

Bess held onto the phone. 'Kirstie, this is important.'

'You guys are always off doing something important,' Kirstie said. 'And you've *never* asked for my help. Not even once.'

'This is not something you can help with, Kirstie.'

Kirstie snatched the phone out of Bess's hand. 'Jarli,' she said. 'Are you gonna save the town or what?'

Bess could hear Jarli's voice: 'I don't have time for this, Kirstie.'

'Whatever you're doing, you need all the help you can get,' Kirstie said. 'Tell me what's going on, or I'm putting Mum on.'

'Look, I'm sorry we never invited you to join us on our thrilling adventures,' Jarli said sarcastically, 'but unless you know how to find out which plane the defence minister is on, you can't help us this time.'

'He's on flight CA 215,' Kirstie said.

Jarli and Bess both fell silent, stunned.

'Are you joking?' Bess asked finally.

'No,' Kirstie said.

'How could you possibly know that?'

'My UFO forum. One group keeps track of flight path data. Whenever a member sees a politician at an airport—somebody who might be involved in a cover-up—they take note of which plane they got on.'

'That sounds like a security risk for the government,' Jarli said.

'A massive one, yeah. But the more they try to silence the conspiracy theorists, the more it looks like a conspiracy. Anyway, someone saw Aaron Fisher get on flight CA 215 about twenty minutes ago.'

'Wow,' Bess said.

Kirstie raised an eyebrow. 'So. Anything else you need?'

'Uh, no,' Jarli said. 'That was it.'

'Well, come here as soon as you can. I'm bored, and the wi-fi here sucks.' Kirstie tossed the phone back to Bess, poked her tongue out and disappeared into the hotel room.

Bess put the phone to her ear. 'Your sister is amazing.'

'I know,' Jarli said. 'But don't tell her that—you'll never hear the end of it.'

PART THREE: INCURSION

I'M GOING TO STOP UPDATING *TRUTH*. I'M NOT SURE THE WORLD SHOULD HAVE A LIE-DETECTOR APP.

I CAN'T ERASE IT—OTHER PEOPLE HAVE ALREADY COPIED MY CODE AND MADE THEIR OWN VERSIONS. BUT I CAN STOP CONTRIBUTING TO THE PROBLEM.

A FRIEND ONCE TOLD ME THAT TRUST IS MORE IMPORTANT THAN TRUTH. I'VE FINALLY REALISED SHE WAS RIGHT.

—From the documentation for Truth, *final version*

EIGHTY-SEVEN PER CENT

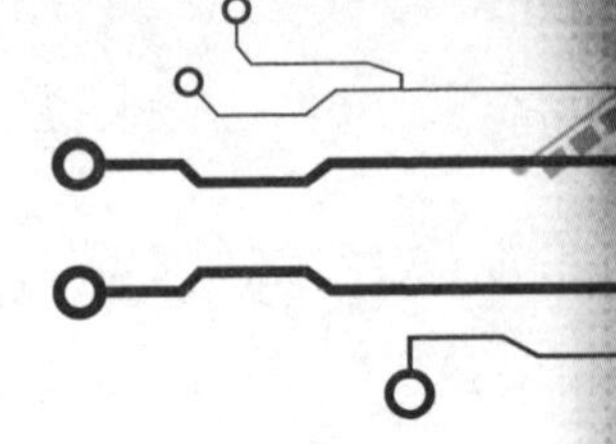

The pouring rain made it hard for Anya to see the drone until it had almost reached the window. It had no lights—it was just a menacing silhouette, hovering over the street like a giant dragonfly. Its wingspan was almost two metres across. She wasn't even sure how it stayed in the air.

A satchel dangled from a hook under the chassis. Anya leaned out the window to get it. As she did, she looked down. The robot was still outside the door, waiting with infinite patience. Ready to zap anyone who came out.

Anya unhooked the bag and pulled it inside. The drone beeped cheerfully and zipped away into the clouds.

Plowman was coming up the stairs. Anya held up the bag. 'I got it. Let's see what Jarli has prepared.'

When she saw what was inside, her heart sank. Two pairs of dorky glasses with no lenses. The frames were covered with spots and blotches. When Anya picked them up, they weren't even plastic. They had been printed on thick paper, then folded into shape.

Plowman took one pair. Some of the light came back into his eyes as he examined them. 'Hmm. Not bad, Jarli.'

'Eaton does not even wear glasses,' Anya objected. 'How will these fool the robot into thinking we are her?'

'Machines don't "see" the way you or I do,' Plowman said. 'These spots are digital signals for the camera. Jarli must have found some photos of Eaton's face—probably on other people's social media feeds—and converted them into a pattern the machine can understand.' He put the glasses on. 'You were right. He is a genius. Although he wouldn't have had time to write the conversion script himself. He must have modified—'

'Are you really saying that wearing these will stop the robot from shooting us?' Anya interrupted. She put the flimsy paper glasses on her nose.

'One study showed that glasses like these were capable of fooling a computer eighty-seven per cent of the time.'

'How reassuring.'

'There's only one way to be certain,' Plowman said. 'Come on.'

Anya pressed her ear to the door. She couldn't hear the robot outside—but that didn't mean it wasn't there. Machines didn't need to breathe or adjust cramped limbs.

'Remember,' Plowman said. 'You have to be facing the robot for the glasses to fool it. Don't turn your back on it.'

'Will it not be suspicious when it sees *two* Vipers?' Anya asked.

'I'm hoping it's not that smart.'

Hoping, Anya thought. *Great.*

'I will go first,' she said.

'What? Why?'

'I am useless in here. You are not. If the robot zaps me, close the door before it gets you. You can help Jarli using your drones, or your money.'

Plowman nodded slowly. 'OK. Good luck.'

Anya turned back to the door, trying not to feel disappointed. She realised she had been hoping he might object. *No, Anya, you're just a kid. I'll go first.*

She touched the glasses on her nose, checking that they were properly in place. They still didn't feel like much protection. Then she opened the door.

It was hard not to scream. The robot was right in front of her, poised to attack. It levelled its mouth-spike, ready to spray her with anaesthetic—

But it didn't fire.

Anya edged forwards. The robot stepped backwards, then forwards, then back again, like it was trying to dance with her. The gleaming eyes were fixed on her face. It thought she was Viper.

She breathed out, slowly. 'It is not attacking,' she said, trying not to move her lips too much. She didn't quite understand how Jarli's trick had worked, and didn't want to disrupt it.

Anya circled slowly around the robot, keeping her head turned towards it. It scuttled around to face her, until it saw Plowman in the doorway, then it swung back towards him.

Two Vipers, Anya thought. Would the robot realise it had been tricked?

Then she realised there was a problem. The doorway was too dark, and Plowman was taller than her. His body was visible, but his face was drenched in shadow. Anya couldn't see his glasses. The robot probably couldn't see them either.

'Step forward!' she told Plowman. 'Into the light!'

As if it had heard her, the robot trotted towards Plowman, blocking the doorway. He couldn't step out.

'Shut the door!' Anya yelled.

The handle was on the same side as Plowman's broken arm. He tried to reach across his body with the other and grab the door. Too late.

The robot sprayed his face with anaesthetic. Plowman screamed, clutching at his eyes. The robot stepped forward, stopping the door from closing. It raised a claw and zapped him with its stun gun.

Plowman crumpled to the ground.

'No!' Anya cried.

The robot swivelled to face her. Anya backed away, forcing herself to keep looking at the robot. Every instinct told her to turn and run.

After a few seconds, the robot lost interest in her. It turned, stepped over Plowman's body and scuttled inside, out of sight. The door swung closed behind it.

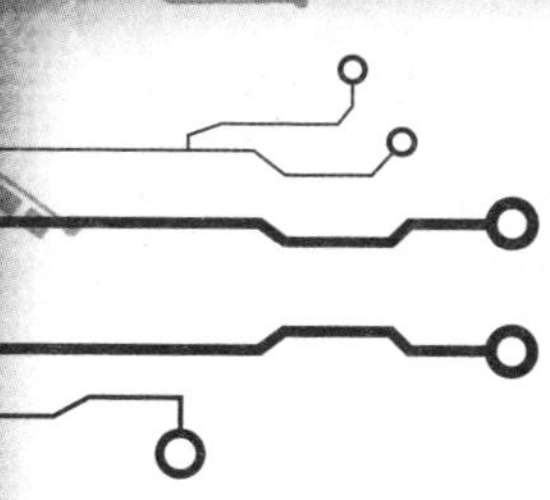

SHHH . . .

Jarli ran.

His breaths were ragged and his legs ached. His eyes burned from sweat and exhaustion. The rain made his clothes heavy. But he didn't dare slow down. Only forty-five minutes until Viper's deadline, and he had a lot of ground to cover.

After Kirstie had given him the flight number, he'd checked Viper's map. He and Bess calculated that at exactly noon, if the plane didn't change its flight path, it would be passing over Kelton.

Specifically, the cliffs above the lake.

It was perfect for Viper's launch. ISOLATED. Close to Eaton's office at the school, and one of the highest points in Kelton.

It was also where Cobra had nearly killed Jarli, a year ago. Where all this had begun—and where it would all end, one way or the other.

Apparently Dana Reynolds had shamed the defence minister out of dropping the bomb. That had bought some time. But it made Jarli the only one left who could stop Viper.

Jarli reached the edge of his school oval, jumped over the fence and landed in front of the trees. He looked around. No sign of Viper—she was probably already up on the clifftop.

He had brought three things from Viper's surgery.

A battery-powered bone saw, hopefully loud enough to distract Viper and lure her away from the botulism canister.

A toxic waste disposal bag he could wrap the canister in.

An air filtration mask, which might protect him from the toxin if he failed. Maybe. Probably not.

Jarli suddenly saw a figure sprinting across the oval towards him. Anya.

Jarli took off his mask and left it dangling around his neck. 'What are you doing here?' he asked, as Anya jumped over the fence like an Olympic hurdler.

'Bess told me you would be here,' she puffed.

'You were supposed to get out of town. With Plowman and your Dad.'

Anya hesitated. 'Plowman is unconscious in the alley next to the prison,' she said finally. 'The robot got him, and I couldn't carry him here.'

Jarli felt a stab of guilt. His glasses trick hadn't worked. Because of him, Plowman was still trapped.

Anya continued, 'My father . . . he drowned when

the tunnel flooded.'

Jarli gaped. 'What?!'

She wouldn't meet his gaze. 'So, I thought you could use some backup.'

Jarli flashed back to the tunnel. The dark, the cold, the roaring water. He had come so close to drowning himself. It was impossible not to imagine what Scanner's last moments had been like.

'I'm so sorry, Anya.' Jarli touched her arm, but Anya shook his hand off.

'There is not much time,' she said. 'What is the plan?'

Jarli cleared his throat. 'I think Viper is at the top of that hill. She'll want to launch the canister right before the minister's plane flies over at twelve. I'm going to switch this on and leave it somewhere.' He held up the bone saw. 'Then, while she's distracted by the noise, I'll try to get past her, grab the canister and wrap it in these bags so the toxin is sealed in.'

'Let me take the saw,' Anya said. 'We can split up. I'll switch on the saw when you are in position on the other side of her. Then you can sneak up behind her to get the canister.'

Jarli nodded. That did sound better. 'OK. Use this button here to turn on the saw.'

'Even if we stop her from releasing the botulism, she may still shoot us in the back as we run away.'

'She might,' Jarli agreed. 'Do you have a better idea?'

He genuinely hoped she would say yes. But Anya thought about it and shook her head. 'No. Let's do this.'

They crept up the hill, weaving through the trees. The canopy kept the rain off them, but it still trickled down the trunks, turning the dirt to mud, which sucked hungrily at Jarli's shoes.

Anya grabbed his shoulder.

'What?' he asked.

'Shhh.'

Jarli looked around. He couldn't see anything except trees and wet mist.

'Sorry,' Anya said finally. 'I thought I heard something.'

'Might have been Viper,' Jarli whispered. 'I think we're close.'

He turned to keep walking—

And then something snapped closed around his ankle.

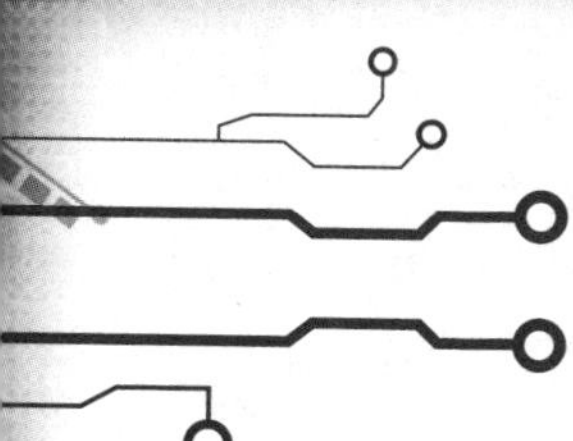

OLDER THAN HIS FACE

Jarli screamed as a loop of steel wire yanked his feet out from under him. He dropped the waste bags as he slammed into the mud. The wire dragged him sideways and pulled him up into the air.

Within seconds he was dangling upside-down from his ankle, two or three metres above the ground. The trees swayed dizzyingly around him. His phone fell out of his pocket and landed in the mud. His ankle was in agony.

'Anya!' he cried.

She was directly below him, eyes wide. 'A trap!'

'You think?! Get me out of this!'

'Viper must have set it up, in case someone figured out where she was planning to launch from. So she could—'

'Give me the saw! So I can cut myself free!' It was designed to cut bone. Jarli hoped it would be strong enough to slice through the steel cable.

Anya raised the saw, but she was too short. Jarli couldn't reach it. She tossed the saw into the air and Jarli grabbed for it, but he missed. He'd never tried to catch something upside down before. Anya somehow caught the falling saw without losing any fingers.

Jarli reached for it. 'Try again.'

Anya stopped talking, scanning the forest around her. Jarli couldn't see what she was looking at, and because he was spinning slowly in the air, soon he couldn't see her either. All the blood had rushed to his head.

By the time he'd done a full circle, Anya was gone. So was the saw. Jarli's phone lay alone in the mud.

'Anya?' Jarli hissed. 'Anya!'

The only sound was the rain against the canopy.

The loop was cutting into Jarli's ankle. He tried to do a sit up, but he couldn't reach it. The other end of the rope was threaded through a pulley which dangled from a branch about a metre above his feet. The tree trunk looked barely thick enough to support his weight, but he couldn't reach it.

As he slowly spun, helpless, he realised someone was standing between the trees nearby. It was his father.

'Dad!' Jarli yelled. 'Help me!'

A grin spread across Dad's face. 'Oh my,' he said. 'Isn't this convenient?'

Not Dad, Jarli realised. *Cobra.*

'Do have any idea how much trouble you've caused me?' Cobra circled Jarli slowly, looking up at him. Jarli was spinning, so Cobra crossed his field of view over and over, his voice seeming to come from all around. Cobra was taller than Anya. He could reach Jarli if he wanted.

'I'm really sorry,' Jarli said, frantically racking his brain for a plan. 'If you cut me down, I can help you.'

His phone beeped from the mud below. LIE

Cobra laughed—a short, sharp bark. 'It was so hard to avoid getting caught out by that damned app. But I usually managed it, unlike you. To be honest, you're less truthful than I am.' He grinned broadly, showing long, yellow teeth. His gums were receding—a reminder that he was older than his face.

'How did you find me?' Jarli asked, stalling for time.

'I called Viper. I confessed that I'd lost you. I expected him to be angry. I thought he might even kill me. But he just laughed.'

Jarli realised that Cobra didn't know who Viper was. Eaton had carefully hidden her true identity even from those who worked for her. Jarli knew something that Cobra didn't—but he wasn't sure how to turn that to his advantage.

'Apparently, Viper messed around in your brain a little bit.' Cobra reached behind his back and pulled out a machete. 'And while he was in there, he implanted something. A poison capsule, just like I have. But it also functions as a tracker. He told me exactly where you were.'

Jarli's skin crawled. Viper already knew he was here. And she could kill him with the push of a button.

Cobra reached up and grabbed Jarli by the hair. Jarli yelped. Cobra's eyes were focused on Jarli's forehead, like he could see through the bone to the brain beneath.

'I wonder what Viper needed you to forget?' Cobra mused.

Jarli already knew. Plowman had told him who Viper was, and Viper had erased the information.

'Just tell me what you want,' Jarli said.

Cobra released him, and Jarli swung back. He felt like he was going to VOMIT. His swollen foot had gone numb.

'Me?' Cobra said. 'I want you dead. I'd cut your throat right now. But Viper doesn't want that. "No unnecessary casualties", he told me.'

Jarli thought back to Eaton's face. Cold. Merciless. But apparently not a psychopath. Not like Cobra.

'So you and me are gonna take a quick road trip,'

Cobra said. 'I parked your dad's new car down at the school. We'll seal up the windows and doors, then drive out of town while Viper is dispersing the toxin. But I don't want you to escape again.' He wiped some rainwater off the giant blade with his T-shirt.

'You're cutting me down,' Jarli said hopefully. 'Right?'

Cobra's grin widened. 'Something like that.' He grabbed Jarli's hair and pulled downwards, bending the tree branch and bringing Jarli's ankle within reach. Jarli screamed as Cobra raised the machete—

And then a whining, buzzing sound filled the air. The bone saw.

Cobra let go of Jarli and whirled around. The branch sprang back into place, bouncing Jarli sickeningly upwards.

'Who's there?' Cobra demanded. 'Show yourself!'

There was no answer from the forest. But Jarli knew who it must be. Anya, distracting Cobra so Jarli could get away.

Again, Jarli tried to fold himself in half so he could grab the loop. Again, he couldn't reach.

Then the tree lurched. Suddenly Jarli realised what Anya was doing—cutting through the trunk with the saw.

'What the—' Cobra began.

The tree fell. Jarli covered his head with his arms as the ground rushed up to meet him. He hit the mud and rolled sideways just in time to avoid the trunk, which crashed down after him.

'Run, Jarli!' Anya yelled. Now he could see her, on the other side of the fallen tree. 'Get to Viper! Stop her!'

Cobra snarled and swung the machete at Anya. She side-stepped. It whipped through the air, hitting nothing.

Jarli was already frantically tugging at the loop around his ankle. Without his weight pulling on it, he was able to loosen the cable. It finally came off, leaving an angry red line around his ankle.

He snatched a glance back at Anya. She was keeping Cobra busy, dancing around him like a pro boxer.

Jarli wanted to help her. But she was right. If he didn't stop Viper, they would both be dead soon.

'Go!' she shouted.

Jarli snatched up the toxic waste bags and ran, up the hill towards the falls.

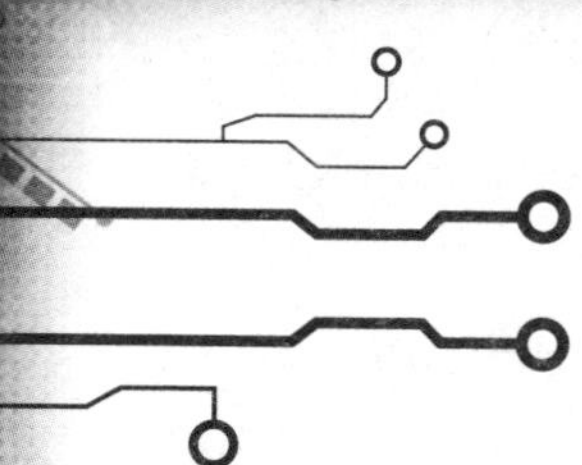

KNIFE TO A FIST FIGHT

Roaring like a lion, Cobra stabbed at Anya's chest with the machete.

Anya stepped aside just in time. The blade swung past, slicing the sleeve of her top.

As she dodged, she aimed a punch just under Cobra's ribs. It connected, but the angle was wrong. He barely reacted. It was like punching a rhino.

'Give up,' she told him. She knew he wouldn't—but she wanted him to be angry. Angry people made mistakes.

Teeth clenched, Cobra raised the machete above Anya's head and brought it down quickly, like a lightning strike. Anya jumped backwards. The point of the blade whipped past the tip of her nose, missing her by centimetres.

'Old man,' she said. 'You have already lost.'

This wasn't true. He had brought a knife to a fist fight. It was Anya who would lose. But she could buy Jarli some time. Give him a chance to save the town.

'Die!' Cobra bellowed, and slashed sideways at her neck.

Anya ducked. The machete skimmed the top of her hair and then thunked into the tree beside her head.

Cobra yanked on the handle, trying to wrench the blade free. But it was wedged in deep. He would be defenceless for two or three seconds.

Make them count, Anya told herself.

She raised her leg and kicked Cobra three times. First in the knee, then the arm, then the face, all with the same foot—*bam, bam, bam!*

He stumbled backwards, but the machete came with him, popping out of the tree trunk with a *crack.* Blood poured from his broken nose.

He raised the **MACHETE.**

Anya was exhausted. There was no way she could win this. She was going to die. Like her sister. Like her father. Like all those others left in Viper's terrible wake.

But she had to stall Cobra as long as possible. For Jarli. For Kelton.

Her fists felt so heavy. She raised them anyway.

'Do you surrender yet?' she asked.

Cobra spat some blood on the ground and charged, holding the weapon up like an Olympic torch.

Anya braced herself, ready to feint one way and then dodge the other—

Then Cobra tripped over nothing. His legs just collapsed beneath him.

The machete tumbled out of his hand, and he flopped into the mud.

Anya hovered, uncertain whether to attack or to run away.

Cobra tried to get up. But it looked like his arms and legs wouldn't obey.

'No,' he gasped. He was starting to dribble. 'You can't!'

His right hand shook, and Anya saw a faint orange glow under the skin.

'Why?' Cobra moaned.

Footsteps were thumping through the bush somewhere. Someone else was coming. Anya didn't take her eyes off Cobra. Eventually he stopped twitching and lay still, his face frozen in an agonised grimace.

Former Constable Blanco ran into the clearing. She took in the fallen tree, the machete, the phone in the mud and Cobra's body. Then she looked at Anya. 'What happened?'

Anya wasn't sure if Blanco could be trusted. 'What are you doing here?'

Blanco spoke quickly. 'Dana Reynolds called me.

We've been working together to expose Viper. Where is she?'

Jarli's phone didn't beep, so Anya took a chance. 'She's at the top of the hill, we think,' she said. 'Jarli went after her. We have to move quickly—but watch out for traps.'

THREADING THE RIGHT CELLS TOGETHER

Jarli sprinted up the hill, dodging trees and rocks as he raced towards the falls. Without Anya, and without the bone saw, he had no way to distract Viper. He didn't even have his phone to call for backup.

He would just have to hope. Hope he could sneak past Viper. Hope he could get the botulism canister before she loaded it onto the rocket. Wrap it in the waste bags, run, and hope she wouldn't catch him.

Soon the trees thinned. Black clouds blocked out the sun. Rain slashed sideways across the cliffs. The lake below had turned into a deadly whirlpool. The water must still be draining into the tunnels underneath.

The rocket was right at the edge of the cliff. It was almost as tall as Jarli himself, with fat boosters at the bottom and a sleek point at the top. The botulism canister was already fixed to it with taut nylon straps. Ready to fill the air with death, killing the defence minister, and anyone left in Kelton.

The buckles and straps looked straightforward enough. But Viper was standing right next to the rocket, her eyes on the grey sky. She had a phone in one hand and a gun in the other. Could he undo the straps without her seeing him?

Maybe he could push the rocket off the cliff. That might save the minister. But it might also poison Kelton's water supply with botulism. And when the water evaporated, who knew where the TOXIC CLOUD would end up?

Jarli edged sideways so he could approach the rocket without entering Viper's line of sight. Then he started creeping up the slope towards the rocket. He tried not to get too close to the cliff edge. If he fell into that whirlpool, he would get sucked into the tunnels and drown, or be smashed against the deadly rock walls.

He was out of the trees now. About ten metres away from Viper. Completely exposed. He kept his eyes on her. She hadn't moved.

Five metres to go.

Four.

Then Viper turned around and levelled her gun at him. 'That's close enough.'

Jarli looked at the phone in her other hand, and remembered the tracker chip in his brain. His heart sank. He had been doomed from the start.

'Put those down,' Viper said.

Jarli dropped the toxic waste bags.

'Kick them away.'

Jarli nudged them with his foot. The wind picked them up, blowing them over the edge of the cliff. They floated down to the lake and disappeared into the whirlpool.

Now he had nothing to wrap the canister in. The plan wouldn't work. Kelton was doomed.

'I'm glad you're OK,' Viper said. 'I was worried that I hadn't killed Cobra in time.'

Jarli said nothing, his mind racing.

'I told him not to kill you,' Viper continued, 'but I didn't trust him. He was a brute. I always knew I'd have to get rid of him eventually.' She gestured to the air filter dangling around Jarli's neck. 'You'd better put that on.'

'Where's your mask?' Jarli asked.

'I told you I was leaving Kelton.' Viper glanced up at the sky, looking for the plane. 'This is me, leaving.'

Jarli glanced at the rocket. From here he could see the numbers on the control panel, counting down to the launch. The canister had its own control panel and screen, counting down to the release of the toxin. The time was 11:54. The rocket would launch in five minutes. The canister would open a minute after that.

Maybe Jarli could hack the control panel on the rocket, or the canister. But Viper would shoot him if he got any closer. His only chance was to talk her out of it.

He couldn't lie, though. She had his app on her phone.

'I understand why you're doing this,' he said. True.

Viper didn't lower the gun. 'You do, huh?'

'Your whole unit was wiped out overseas. They died because the defence minister knew a source was unreliable, and didn't tell anyone.'

'Not just my unit,' Viper said. 'His career is a long list of selfish mistakes. Every time he screws up, good people die. I assume the only reason he didn't kill both of us with that thermobaric warhead is that Reynolds shamed him out of it.'

'Poisoning him won't bring your friends back.'

'Imagine someone murdered your family.' Viper turned her face to the sky, looking for the plane. 'And Bess, and Anya, and Doug, and anyone else you care about. Would you be willing to let that go? Just because you *couldn't bring them back?*'

The thought left a chill in Jarli's chest. 'Of course not. I'd want the killer arrested. But I wouldn't—'

'Arrested.' Viper snorted. 'You don't think I tried that? I told my story to the police, and then the media. But Fisher has powerful friends. No-one did anything. Eventually he sent some goons to my house to threaten me. They said if I kept talking, I'd find myself in a lead-lined bag at the bottom of the ocean. So I moved to this little town in the middle of nowhere. I let Fisher think I had given up. Then I started playing by his rules.'

'If you do this, innocent people will die,' Jarli said. 'Everyone else on the plane, everyone left in Kelton . . .'

Viper looked unmoved. 'Like I said. Playing by his rules.'

'You could have told your story to Dana Reynolds,' Jarli said, clutching at straws. 'She confronted Fisher about Malburse when he visited Kelton.'

'Too little, too late. And when she accused him of running a secret government prison, Fisher blamed his deputy and managed to keep his job—*again*. He always avoids punishment. But not today.' Viper checked the countdown. Jarli followed her gaze. Two minutes until the rocket launch. Three minutes until the botulism was released.

'The next defence minister will find out what happened to the last one, and why,' Viper said. 'Maybe he or she will treat their soldiers with more respect.'

'Or maybe all veterans will be worse off,' Jarli

challenged. 'Did you think of that? They'll get blamed for what you're doing right now—' He broke off. Suddenly this all felt familiar.

'Have we already had this conversation?' he asked. 'I found out who you were, tried to convince you not to do this—and then you erased my memory.'

'No,' Viper said. 'I didn't remove your memories. I gave you new ones. The procedure isn't so different.'

Jarli's eyes widened. 'What do you mean?'

'You know how I funded all this.' Viper waved the gun at the rocket and the canister. 'Criminals pay me a fortune to give them new faces and new identities. I chip them as well, so they're forced to do whatever I want. Recommend me to their associates. Spy on my enemies. Hack into police databases. Even steal weapons, cash, rockets. But thanks to your lie-detector app, having a new face isn't enough to disappear. You need to *believe* that you're a new person, otherwise the app will catch you out.'

Jarli was starting to feel sick, but he didn't know why. 'I don't understand.'

'You were on the run from the police,' Viper said. 'You came to me. You wanted a new face, a new identity, and some new memories to make them work. You were about the same size and build as a kid I knew. A kid named Jarli Durras.'

The ground seemed to be shuddering beneath

Jarli's feet. 'This is another one of your tricks.'

'So I modified your face to make you look like Jarli,' Viper continued. 'I kidnapped him. I used an fMRI to find the relevant memories in his head. Then I used a neurosurgical robot to duplicate them in yours—just a matter of threading the right cells together. I sent you home to his family, who didn't suspect a thing. Neither did you. Cobra was supposed to watch you, make sure that the new memories stuck.'

'You're lying!' Jarli shouted, his heart pounding.

'The real Jarli Durras is dead,' Viper said. 'I left him on my surgical table. Check your app.'

Jarli instinctively reached into his pocket. But his phone was still somewhere down the hill, in the mud.

Viper held up her phone. The app was open on her screen. The screen said:

'You are a convicted arsonist named Jackson Leach,' she said, 'who came to me for a new identity. Jarli Durras is dead.'

The phone thought about that for a second.

TRUE

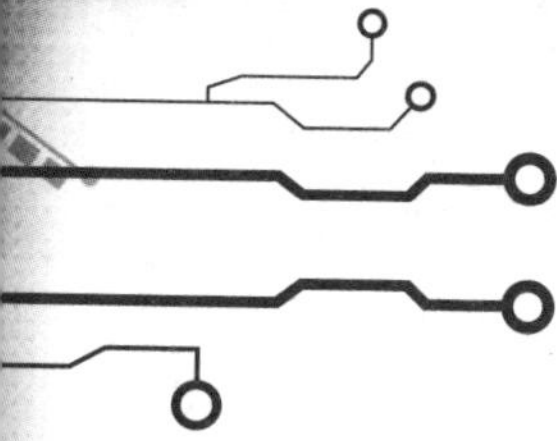

A WORLD-ENDING EXPLOSION

The countdown on the rocket ticked away the seconds.

01:05.

01:04.

'Put that mask on,' Viper said again. 'You may not be the real Jarli, but that doesn't mean you have to die.'

She must be lying, Jarli thought. But it was still right there on the screen: *True*. He tasted blood at the back of his throat, like he'd tried to swallow something sharp.

Viper's story fit all the facts. The scar on his head. The body in her surgical room. It explained why she'd given Jarli brain surgery instead of killing him, and why she'd planted Cobra in his house.

'Why are you telling me this?' Jarli's voice came out as a hoarse whisper.

'There's no point lying to each other now, is there?' Viper said. 'This will all be over in a minute.'

Less than that. The rocket launch was fifty-five

seconds away. But that barely seemed to matter now.

Noises in the trees, somewhere behind him. Someone was coming. Maybe Anya. Jarli was suddenly ashamed. He didn't want to see her. She was good, and he was bad.

Jarli wasn't himself. He was *dead*. He'd been dead for weeks.

The thought snagged in his brain. *Weeks.*

'How did you preserve the body?' he asked.

Viper raised an eyebrow. '*That's* your question?'

'I've had the scar on my head for two weeks,' Jarli said. 'That body looked no more than a few days old.'

'And you're an expert?'

'According to you, yes. I'm a criminal.'

Viper sighed. 'Fine. I froze Jarli's body. I took it out this morning to make room in the freezer for the botulism. Happy now?'

She held up her phone. The app said **TRUE**

Except . . .

'That's *Truth Premium,*' Jarli said. 'You made it. It's programmed to trust your voice print, no matter what you say.'

Viper's eyes narrowed. 'That doesn't mean I'm lying.'

'No. But you're a master manipulator.' It was all coming together in Jarli's head. 'You *tried* to replace me with a criminal doppelganger, but the surgery killed him.'

'Wrong.' But Viper looked uneasy now.

'This is what you do,' Jarli continued. 'You trick people. Earlier today you convinced Plowman he was Viper, and now you're trying to convince me that I'm not me.'

'You're not,' Viper said, teeth clenched. She was nervous.

'So I get distracted. So I don't . . .' Jarli trailed off. *So I don't what?*

He looked at the launch countdown.

00:26.

00:25.

He took a step towards the rocket.

Viper levelled the gun at him. 'Back off.'

'You don't want to shoot me,' Jarli said. 'Because I'm just a kid, and your only target is Aaron Fisher. You'll say anything to stop me from interfering with that rocket.'

Viper gritted her teeth. 'You're right. I don't *want* to shoot you. But I will, if you make me.'

00:19.

00:18.

'I don't think so.' Jarli took another step towards the rocket.

Bang!

The gunshot echoed across the clifftop.

Viper's head snapped backwards. Her body went instantly limp. She toppled off the edge of the cliff. Her body hit the water seconds later with a distant *splash,* and was sucked down into the whirlpool.

Jarli whirled around. He saw former Constable Blanco running up the hill towards him with a gun in her hand. Anya was right behind her. Dana Reynolds followed them, holding up a camera.

'Jarli,' Blanco yelled. 'Are you all right?'

There was no time to answer her question. No time to wonder if Viper really would have shot him. No time to hack the rocket controls before the launch.

00:03.

00:02.

Jarli grabbed the nylon straps which held the canister and the rocket together. He held on tight.

There was a world-ending explosion beneath his feet, and suddenly Jarli was shooting into the sky.

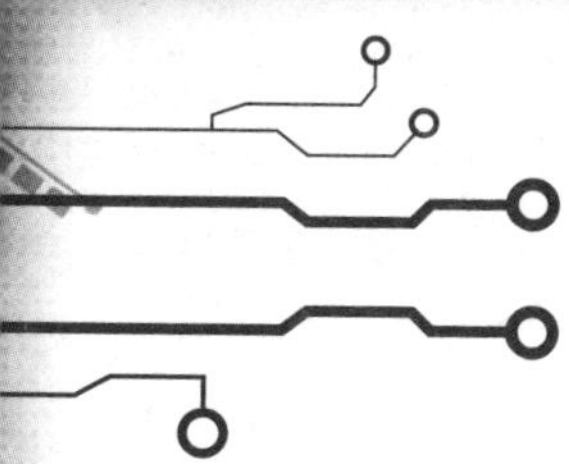

INCORRECT PASSWORD

Jarli's shoes were burning. They were right next to the rocket's thrusters, which made a deafening roar. The clifftop was getting smaller and smaller down below as the rocket zoomed up towards the dark, wet clouds. The vibrations made Jarli's teeth rattle.

The screen on the rocket was blinking furiously as it clocked the altitude. 100 METRES. 150 METRES. 200 METRES. 250 METRES.

Jarli had no parachute. No safe spot to land. There was no way he could survive this. But he could save Kelton.

The wind blasted him as he leaned sideways, trying to get a look at the control panel for the botulism canister. Fifty-six seconds left on the clock. That was how long he had to figure out how to stop it from opening.

900 METRES. 950 METRES. 1000 METRES.

As the rocket shot higher and higher into the sky, Jarli let go of the straps with one hand so he could operate the control panel with the other.

But shifting his weight made the rocket tilt back towards him, changing its trajectory. If he wasn't careful, he could accidentally steer the rocket back down into the ground, where it would probably explode, showering the town with deadly particles.

Jarli wrapped his legs around the rocket, like it was a horse. Keeping his chest pressed against it, he reached for the control panel again with one hand.

The screen said:

TIME UNTIL RELEASE: 00:44.

Under that, there was a button which said, CANCEL.

Relieved, Jarli stabbed the button. A message flashed up on the screen:

PASSWORD REQUIRED:_____________________

Jarli felt the blood drain from his face. *Oh, no*. He was strapped to a rocket which was hurtling into the sky with a payload of the most dangerous substance in the world. And the only person who knew the password to stop it was DEAD.

00:32.

00:31.

The air was getting thinner as the rocket approached the stratosphere. Jarli was getting dizzy. His muscles were weakening. The altitude clock said: 4900 METRES. 4950 METRES. 5000 METRES.

There was no 'forgot password' option. The rocket was shaking, making it impossible to keep his hand steady. It took Jarli several seconds to type ADMIN.

The screen flashed red. INCORRECT PASSWORD.

He tried PASSWORD.

INCORRECT PASSWORD.

00:24.

00:23.

The rocket was above the clouds now. Jarli could see the sun, sudden and blinding. The wind was freezing against his wet skin. He was struggling to breathe up here. If he blacked out, he would fall to his death—and then the toxin would kill everybody else.

Teeth chattering, Jarli racked his brain for everything he knew about Viper.

VIPER. INCORRECT PASSWORD.

EATON. INCORRECT PASSWORD.

MARIA. INCORRECT PASSWORD.

MARIAEATON. INCORRECT PASSWORD.

FISHER. INCORRECT PASSWORD.

AARONFISHER. INCORRECT PASSWORD.

Jarli screamed with frustration. The blasting wind stole his voice.

00:11.

00:10.

Darkness crawled in from the edges of his vision. He needed *air*.

The rocket was slowing down. As it slowly spun, Jarli saw a speck on the horizon—Fisher's plane.

00:08.

00:07.

The plane was about the same altitude as the rocket—8400 metres, according to the screen. The rocket was probably supposed to fly higher, but Jarli was weighing it down. Not enough to save the plane, though. The canister was going to dump the botulism right in front of it.

00:06.

00:05.

Fisher would die. Finally Viper would get her revenge for all those dead—

Wait!

Suddenly inspired, Jarli started typing again. The nickname of a dead soldier Viper had told him about a year ago.

00:04.

00:03.

Jarli typed: NURSINGHOME.

A message flashed up: ARE YOU SURE YOU WANT TO CANCEL?

Jarli frantically stabbed the *YES* button.

RELEASE CANCELLED.

Jarli stared at the screen. He couldn't believe it. He'd done it. He'd saved everybody.

Except himself.

The boosters sputtered and died. The rocket hung in the air for a moment, and then began to fall. From nine kilometres up.

TERMINAL VELOCITY

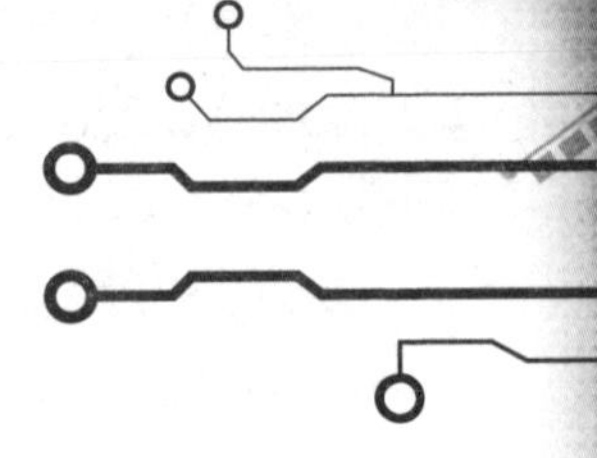

It was like the first drop on a rollercoaster. Jarli kept thinking the rocket had reached maximum speed, only to have it plummet even faster. He fought to hang onto the nylon straps with his freezing hands as it hurtled towards oblivion at almost 300 kilometres per hour. The terror was sickening.

The defence minister's private jet swept overhead, sending shockwaves through the air and filling it with the roar of jet engines.

Still hugging the dead rocket, Jarli watched the plane shrink away into the mist. He had sacrificed his own life to save the people on that plane. He wondered if they would ever know.

Suddenly the air blasting his face didn't seem so thin. He was getting close to the ground. Not good.

5100 METRES. 5000 METRES. 4900 METRES.

He rested his feet on the stabiliser fins. By shifting his weight, he could steer the rocket, sort of. But not enough to keep it in the air. No matter what he did, it was going to hit the ground. Hard.

The clifftop was 3000 metres below. The rocket was going to crash almost exactly where it had taken off. Maybe Jarli could steer the rocket towards the lake. The impact might still kill him. Even if it didn't, he could drown when he was sucked into the whirlpool. But a slim chance was better than none.

Jarli leaned sideways, holding onto the straps. The rocket's nose tilted towards the lake, slightly changing the angle of descent, still accelerating downwards. 2000 METRES. 1800 METRES.

And then Jarli saw something moving down below. Just a speck, but getting bigger. One of Plowman's giant drones. It was hovering about 300 metres above the clifftop. Still watching over the town.

Jarli threw his weight to the left, trying to steer the rocket towards the drone. The nose of the rocket started to turn. But not far enough. It wasn't going to hit the drone.

1500 METRES. 1300 METRES. 1100 METRES.

Jarli bunched the nylon straps in one hand and tore at the buckles with the other. He couldn't let the botulism canister shatter against the ground, or this would all be for nothing.

Finally he found the correct buckle. The straps loosened, and the canister fell out. It started to drift away, like it was in zero gravity. Jarli stretched out his free hand and caught the canister just before it floated out of reach. He hugged the can of death to his chest like a football.

Still holding the straps with his other hand, he stood up, surfing on the rocket for a moment. 900 METRES. 600 METRES.

Then he jumped.

For a second he flew, legs kicking the empty air. The wind slowed him down, but the rocket was more streamlined, so it kept accelerating downwards, leaving Jarli alone in the sky.

The rocket SLAMMED into the clifftop. Shrapnel flew everywhere. The sharp *bang* reached Jarli a split-second later . . .

And then he hit the drone.

Something snapped inside one of his legs. The drone tipped sideways, engine screaming at the extra weight. Jarli scrabbled for a handhold. He managed to grab one of the wings—

The drone was in a death spiral, turbines screeching—

Jarli fought to hold on—

But the drone dipped under him, rolling him off the wing—

The world spun around him, faster and faster—

The clifftop rushed up—

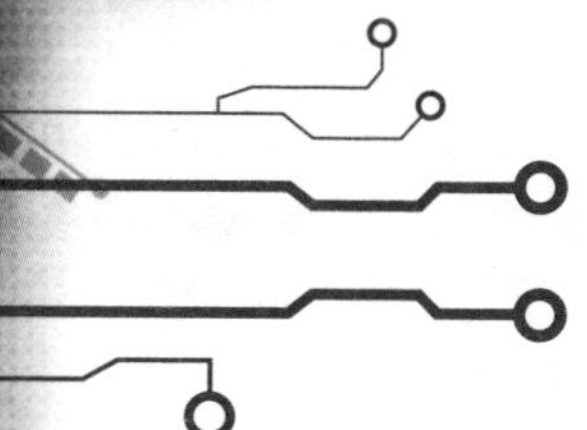

TOO DISTURBING TO AIR

. . . THE BOY, WHO CANNOT BE NAMED FOR LEGAL REASONS, REPORTEDLY DEFUSED A BIOLOGICAL WEAPON IN MID-AIR, SAVING THE SMALL TOWN OF KELTON FROM A POTENTIALLY DEVASTATING ATTACK. POLICE HAVE RECOVERED THE WEAPON, AND SAY IT IS INTACT. TRIBUTES TO THE BOY ARE FLOWING IN FROM . . .

. . . OTHER FOOTAGE TOO DISTURBING TO AIR SHOWS A SCHOOL NURSE HOLDING THE BOY AT GUNPOINT BEFORE SHE IS FATALLY SHOT BY A SUSPENDED POLICE OFFICER. EVIDENCE RECOVERED FROM THE NURSE'S HOME AND OFFICE INDICATE THAT SHE WAS THE CRIMINAL MASTERMIND KNOWN AS VIPER. SHE IS BELIEVED TO BE RESPONSIBLE FOR MURDERS, IDENTITY THEFTS, AND EVEN A PLANE CRASH, ALONG WITH MANY OTHER . . .

. . . AN EXTENSIVE DOSSIER ON THE MINISTER FOR DEFENCE, AARON FISHER, IN VIPER'S OFFICE. FISHER APPEARS TO HAVE BEEN THE TARGET OF THE ATTACK. HE HAS DENIED ALL THE ALLEGATIONS IN THE DOCUMENT,

AND SAYS THE WORDS OF A VIOLENT CRIMINAL SHOULD BE IGNORED. BUT HIS DEPUTY, ASSISTANT MINISTER SANDRA RIZVI HAS MADE A STATEMENT SUPPORTING SOME OF THE ALLEGATIONS.

I'M DANA REYNOLDS, AND YOU'RE WATCHING NATIONWIDE.

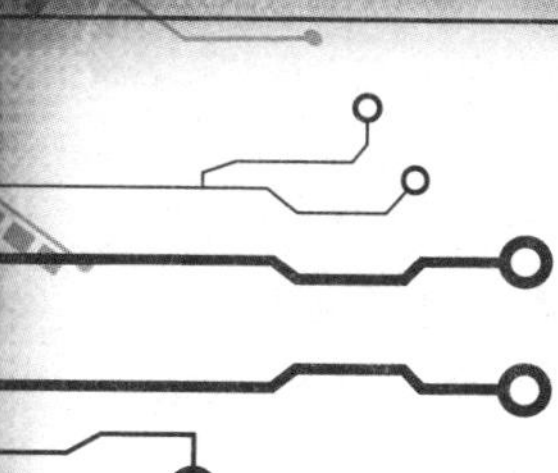

KELTON SAYS GOODBYE

It was the same chapel where Doug's funeral had been held. But this time the coffin was open, and there was a body in it, surrounded by flowers. Hidden speakers played acoustic guitar music. Packets of tissues rested on all the empty seats.

Jarli guessed that Scanner, being an undercover agent a long way from home, probably hadn't had many friends. And since his work undermining Viper hadn't been made public, no strangers had showed up to pay their respects.

Anya saw Jarli and hugged him. She was dry-eyed. 'Thank you for coming.'

'Of course. Mum and Dad are here too, and Kirstie—they're just parking the car. Where should I, uh, sit?'

Anya pointed to where her mum sat alone in the front row. 'Up there, if you like. There is room—and you are family now.'

Jarli nodded, and limped slowly up the aisle. He passed a curly-haired woman with a glittering necklace, and a dour-looking man sweating into his suit. Jarli didn't recognise them, and wondered if they had worked with Scanner. They didn't look like spies, but he supposed that was the point.

Jarli sat near Anya's mum, leaving one chair in between for Anya. Anya's mum wore black and white, like she was an old photograph.

She looked at the medical boot around his foot, and the brace on his broken wrist. 'Jarli, yes?' she said.

Jarli nodded stiffly. 'I'm sorry for your loss.'

'Thank you.'

Bess, her mum and her brother entered through the double doors up the back. Bess beamed at Anya and gave Jarli a cheery wave—with anyone else it would have seemed disrespectful, but as usual, her confidence made it seem OK. When she had visited Jarli at the hospital and seen his foot encased in the moon boot, instead of offering sympathy, she had hefted her crutches and immediately proposed a race through the ward.

Former Constable Blanco arrived next. Plenty of people had said she should be reinstated after shooting Viper and helping to save the town. But others suspected she had worked for Viper, and shot her to stop anyone finding out. The investigation was ongoing. Blanco patted Anya on the shoulder and sat near the back, her expression unreadable.

Finally the rest of Jarli's family arrived. Kirstie sparkled in a sequinned dress. Mum held Dad's arm in a fierce grip—she was never letting him out of her sight again. Dad still looked thin after his stay in Viper's prison.

Detective Zee Arno entered and sat near the back with Blanco. While visiting Jarli in hospital, Arno had updated him on the case. Apparently all Viper's criminal clients had believed they were getting the identities of people she had secretly killed, but Viper had actually imprisoned most of her victims instead. Now they were free—the prisoner transport truck had been found, parked on the side of the highway a few kilometres out of town. This meant all her clients had been suddenly EXPOSED. The police were rounding the last of them up now.

Arno wasn't sure why Viper had kept her victims alive, or freed them afterwards, or even why she had given them real people's identities instead of invented ones. But Jarli thought he understood. Viper had known her clients were evil people. She would have wanted them to be caught after they had served their purpose. She was a villain. But she hadn't seen herself as one.

Jarli wondered why she hadn't put Dad and Doug on the truck with the other prisoners.

Maybe to protect Cobra's cover for a little longer. He supposed he would never know for sure.

Doug entered the chapel with his parents. As long as Jarli had known him, Doug had *always* looked like he was at a funeral. Not today, though. He didn't look happy exactly, but . . . peaceful. Jarli thought that a lot of the anger and sadness Doug seemed to radiate had actually been fear. Now that Viper was dead, his fear was gone. He was a whole new kid, or at least a refurbished one.

Dana Reynolds was last through the door. Jarli hardly recognised her without the thick sheen of makeup. She had no microphone, no camera crew. She nodded to Jarli and sat alone, halfway to the front.

No sign of Plowman. The robot's anaesthetic spray had affected him worse than Doug, causing some complications. But Jarli had seen him at the hospital, and he had been awake at least. He'd even started to talk like his old self. Confident and paranoid at the same time.

Doug and Bess settled in behind Jarli and Anya, leaving their families further back. Doug touched Anya's mother on the arm. 'I'm sorry,' he said. 'Your husband saved my life.'

'Mine too,' Bess added.

Mine too, Jarli thought. It was only because

Scanner had rescued him from Cobra that Jarli had been able to stop Viper. In a way, Scanner was the one who saved the town. It was a shame that so few people were here for his funeral.

Soon a middle-aged woman carried a leather-bound book to a lectern and started making a speech about Scanner's life. His real name had been Rick, and he'd been born in a town called Premiovaya. She told some funny stories from his childhood and the early years of his marriage. She talked about how much he had loved his twin daughters, and his courage when one of them died. Jarli looked at Anya in shock. She didn't take her eyes off the coffin.

The celebrant didn't give many details of Scanner's life after he moved to Kelton. Jarli wondered if she knew why the details were scarce from that point on. He wondered if she knew how many lives he had saved.

But, Jarli remembered, *Scanner also used innocent people as bait to lure Viper out*. The celebrant didn't mention that either. The world was complicated.

Anya's mother approached the lectern and read a poem, her voice cracking. It had been translated into English, so it didn't rhyme. After that, Anya stood up and sang a song, quietly, but perfectly in tune. By the end, tears were streaming down Jarli's cheeks.

Eventually the coffin sank slowly into the floor. The hidden speakers played a pop song from twenty years ago—a favourite from Scanner's youth.

There was no ceremony like this for Cobra. No-one knew who he really was. His body lay unclaimed in the morgue. The doctors said his scars indicated multiple surgeries over many years. Even his old face, the one he had worn when he first met Jarli, hadn't been the original.

Viper didn't get a funeral either. She had no family. Most of the soldiers she'd served with were dead. None of her colleagues from the school were willing to pay for a headstone, and there was no body to bury under it. All of the teachers insisted that they hadn't been friends—they had barely known her.

She was simply gone.

After the funeral, sandwiches and muffins were served in a little function room next to the chapel. The adults sipped coffee and talked in hushed voices.

Jarli's ankle was too sore for him to stand, so he sat on a couch in the corner with a cup of tea. Soon Bess came to join him. Then Anya, then Doug. They all sat together in silence for a while.

'I heard about the offer,' Anya said finally. 'From

the university.'

Jarli hadn't wanted to share this news. Not here. 'How did you hear that?'

Anya smiled, but said nothing.

'What offer?' Bess asked. 'What university? What's going on?'

Jarli cleared his throat. 'The City Institute of Technology offered me a place. They said I can start studying coding there next year, if I want to. I don't even have to finish high school.'

'That's amazing,' Doug said, with a strange smile.

'It's ridiculous,' Jarli said. 'I guess they wanted to get in before any other offers. Use me for publicity, maybe.'

'Are you gonna take it?'

'Of course he's taking it,' Bess said. 'Right?'

Jarli raised his eyebrows. 'And leave you guys? No way!'

'You have to,' Bess said. 'Remember that excursion to the CIT last year? They have the biggest library I've ever seen. If you don't accept, I have no excuse to visit.'

'I'm serious, Bess.'

'So am I. It's only three hours away—we'd see each other all the time.'

Jarli sighed. 'I'll think about it, I guess.'

A pause.

'You know,' Anya said, 'my mother wants to move back to the city.'

'Really?' Bess asked.

'We were only here for Dad's job. She doesn't want to stay.'

'How do you feel about that?'

'Well, I would feel OK about it if Jarli were moving there too.'

Jarli thought about it. With Anya living there and regular visits from Bess, it wouldn't be so lonely. His Mum and Dad had been enthusiastic about the opportunity, when he finally told them. Even Kirstie had sounded proud of him.

'What about you?' Jarli asked Doug. 'Would you visit?'

'No,' Doug said. He still had that strange smile.

'Oh.' Jarli sipped his tea. His disappointment lingered in the air.

'I already accepted my place,' Doug said. 'So I'll be there full time.'

Jarli choked on his tea. Doug laughed.

'Don't look so surprised, Truth Boy. I applied for CIT's robotics course. Maybe they want you for publicity, but they want me for my unparalleled genius.' He slapped Jarli's knee. 'So, are you coming, or what?'

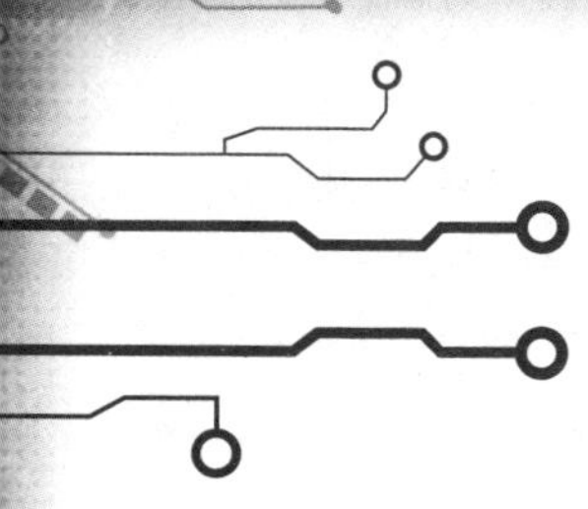

FREEDOM

Maria Eaton watched from her vehicle as the police led Fisher out of the building in handcuffs. The officers were gentle with him. Respectful of his rank. He didn't appear satisfied with this, though. He was red-faced, his hair dishevelled, the buttons through the wrong holes on his shirt. He was blustering, and it looked like the cops were ignoring it. Eaton hoped he would look up and see her through the windscreen, but he didn't.

He wouldn't have recognised her anyway. Blanco's bullet had changed her face. When people saw her, they looked quickly away, but no-one recognised her as Viper.

This was ironic, since the gunshot had widened her mouth and taken a chip out of her tongue. She'd even acquired a hissing lisp. She looked and sounded more like a snake than ever.

It was all fixable, though. Eaton would change her face as soon as she found a new one she liked.

She still wasn't sure exactly how she had survived.

Divine intervention, maybe. Fate. She had woken up on the wet stone floor of an old coal tunnel under Kelton, vomiting water, her face bleeding. She had no memory of the gunshot. She didn't even remember what she had said to the kid on the clifftop.

One cop put a hand on Fisher's head, carefully pushing him down into the back seat of the patrol car. She said something to the other officer, who nodded grimly. Then they climbed in and drove away.

Eaton decided not to follow. She had told the world what she knew about him, and everyone had finally listened. The justice system had eventually worked. Things hadn't gone to plan—both she and Fisher were still alive. But it was enough. She'd had her REVENGE. She had her freedom. She still had money, stored in Plowman's untraceable cryptocurrency. Once she had a replacement identity, a new life was within her grasp.

She wasn't angry anymore. The truth had set her free.

Eaton watched as a young woman walked out of the coffee shop next to Fisher's office and raised her arm, looking for a taxi. Her face was nice and symmetrical, with arched eyebrows and a slightly wide chin.

Yes, Viper thought. *That will do.* She started the engine of the taxi, and drove.

THE END

ACKNOWLEDGMENTS

Thank you to the team at Scholastic Australia for giving me the chance to write this series and for helping it reach its potential. Special thanks to Andrew Berkhut, Lorae Harbottle-Purs, Sarah Hatton, Angie Masters, Chad Mitchell, Claire Pretyman, Cassandra Rathbone and Kate Wenban. It's hard to write 1000 pages in which characters (generally) can't lie. Harder still to set up a twist in book one and reveal it in book five. It would have been impossible without your support.

Thanks to everybody at Simon & Schuster for taking a leap of faith on the series, especially David Gale and Amanda Ramirez.

Thank you to all my friends at Curtis Brown, without whom I couldn't do this for a living. Special thanks to Clare Forster and Benjamin Stevenson.

Thanks to all my friends and family, who read drafts, helped me juggle various life things and played D&D with me whenever I needed a break. There are too many of you to name, but special mentions go to Venetia, Mum, Dad, Beth, Tom, Alice, Chris and Red. Ash, you haven't really helped yet—I'll put you to work when you're older.